My Kind of Girl

Buddhadeva Bose

Translated by Arunava Sinha

Hesperus Worldwide

Hesperus Worldwide
Published by Hesperus Press Limited
19 Bulstrode Street, London W1U 2JN
www.hesperuspress.com

My Kind of Girl first published in Bengali as *Moner Mato Meye* in 1951

This translation first published by Hesperus Press Limited, 2011

My Kind of Girl © Buddhadeva Bose, 1951

Designed and typeset by Fraser Muggeridge studio
Printed in Jordan by Jordan National Press

ISBN: 978-1-84391-856-1

My Kind of Girl

Contents

My Kind of Girl

Chapter One

A bitingly cold night in December. Four passengers sat silently in the first-class waiting room of Tundla station. All four were covered from head to toe, concealed by their overcoats, but even in the dim light of that stark, dispassionate room, built and decorated in accordance with the precise specifications of the Indian Railway, it was obvious that they were very different individuals, thrown together from different corners of society.

The one in the easy chair had an enormously – even indecently – powerful body, as though he were a giant beast, the kind that outgrows their clothes and shoes at sixteen, to the amazement of their parents. His face was large too, almost as big as a jackfruit[1], and longish, on the broad expanse of his cheeks the seeds of next morning's beard – perhaps because his pores were swollen from the cold – already sprouting in blue dots.

The second one was a nicely proportioned, pleasant looking man, dapper, well groomed, immaculate in his western garb; complete with hat, cane and gloves. His face was round, plump, grave, his complexion just the shade of dark that makes good-looking men even better looking; his hair, though plentiful and black, betrayed the occasional flash of silver. His lips were neither too full nor too thin but clearly etched, the kind used to commanding with a few words. Anyone who had set eyes on him would have agreed that rules were never flouted in his disciplined, predictable life, that he never had to raise his voice.

This natural authority in the way he occupied the waiting room chair, legs elegantly crossed, this stateliness, this majestic quality, was also visible in the third person. He was on the stouter side, and of an old-fashioned, aristocratic appearance: hair parted in the middle, ruddy of cheek, with a rakish moustache that suited him perfectly.

But the fourth: he was the antithesis of all this elegance. Slight in build, he was seated in one corner, his feet up on a chair – although a second easy chair was vacant – but there was no sense of repose in the way he reclined. He kept fidgeting but seemed unable to find a comfortable position, and even when he closed his eyes occasionally, furrows appeared on his brow, as though he was thinking of something important and as though volatility of thought was his wont. At first glance he appeared very young; perhaps he was the youngest of the four, but when the light shone on the lower half of his face, you no longer mistook him for a young man.

These four travellers had met earlier that day: in the gardens of the Taj Mahal, on the steps of Sikandra, and again leaving Agra. They had conversed, all in the same compartment, on the train. These exchanges had revealed that the powerfully built man was a contractor; he had been to Delhi to secure a government order, visiting Agra on his way back, and wanted to stop at Varanasi too. The second one was an old, trusted bureaucrat in Delhi, currently in a very high post in the military and off to Allahabad on vital government work, thereafter to Lucknow Cantonment. The third man was one of the better known doctors in Calcutta, Dr Dhar; having delivered a lecture on diphtheria at a medical conference in Delhi, he was now on his way back to tend to his patients. And the fourth was in this part of India simply on holiday; he hadn't decided yet whether to return directly to Calcutta or to stop off some-where along the way. His profession was not clear either; he said he wrote books, but did writing count as a profession? That he was involved with books was clear though, for after the conversation ended, the huge tome he opened seemed, in its form and appearance – so the other three felt – completely unsuitable for casual reading on a train. Whether it was readable at all was suspect.

The bad news had come at Tundla. A goods train had been derailed near Aligarh, no trains were running. How long? Well, it would take at least four or five hours for the lines to be cleared. In other words, no hope tonight? Didn't look like it. The bureaucrat had important work, he had enquired about plane timings – the first flight out was at nine thirty, and yes, he would be able to take a train back to Agra in a bit. The doctor had tried to accept the situation philosophically, but the contractor had kept breathing deeply and muttering, 'So cold... and now!' This despite the fact that both his physique and his clothing were designed to insulate him admirably from plunging temperatures. But the bookish gentleman, the thin one, had been feeling cold indeed; he rubbed his hands together, walked up and down, and then turned around to inform the other three, unnecessarily, that there was no choice but to spend the night in the waiting room.

The four men had just settled down with their luggage, and no one was speaking; all of them were intent on coping with their plight. Even a minute seemed a long while, and they had a long winter night ahead of them.

The contractor shifted in his chair and asked, 'What's the time?' He was wearing a watch, but he directed his question to the others, out of laziness or to use it as a pretext for conversation.

The bureaucrat replied, 'Twelve thirty-five.'

Thirty-five – at least half an hour had been killed since they'd got off the train! The contractor found another question.

'Are there arrangements for sleeping?'

'On the floor?' someone said, dubiously.

The contractor had no objection for his part, but he accepted that the others probably had higher standards, and so, kept going.

'No retiring room here?'

'No.'

It is usually difficult to make progress in a conversation after such monosyllabic replies, but fat people are sociable and gregarious; more words emerged from the depths of the easy chair.

'At least we have seats, think of the other passengers.'

There was no concurring reply, but, as though in response, the sliding doors of the waiting room opened, and cold air immediately filled the room. All four passengers turned their eyes towards the door at this, even that wretched-seeming bookish man, who had been leaning to one side, his eyes shut.

Under the scrutiny of these four pairs of eyes, those who had caused the door to open paused. They were a couple. A young man stood with the door ajar: he was not fully visible but there were hints of a face, its skin chapped by the cold, a home-knitted brown pullover and a cheap pair of trousers. A girl stood by his side, almost nestling against him, even more obscured. She could barely be seen: just a flash of black hair, a proud vermilion streak, a smooth, young-looking neck, white light on her cheek. They stood there for just a few moments, said something softly before they turned and left – but even that seemed to blow a breath of warm air through the wintry waiting room. They were clearly newly-weds, maybe a couple of months in, maybe a year, but they were lost – still – in their love for each other. That slight pause at the door, those soft words exchanged or maybe not exchanged, then their retreat; with all of this they made it amply clear to the middle-aged men that they were still inhabitants of heaven, that as long as they had each other they wanted nothing else, nobody else.

The door was closed again, and all that remained was the heartless, miserly waiting room and four middle-aged men, distraught that the train was not coming, with the lack of comfort, of sleep.

Again, the plump, gregarious man was the first to speak.

'Why did they go back?'

'They didn't look like first-class passengers,' said the doctor.

'No, not because of that,' said the book lover with the furrowed brow, speaking from his corner for the first time since he'd entered the waiting room. 'Not because of that. They went back when they saw us.'

A faint smile appeared on the smooth face of the bureaucrat. 'I see. Honeymoon. In love. Well, tonight at least, they won't be happy.'

'Not at all,' the reader of books replied carelessly. 'They will find a cosy, private spot for themselves, they will enjoy it. They don't want anything else, they just want privacy.'

'Theirs is really that special time of life!' The bureaucrat looked grave as he finished his proclamation. He seemed to be thinking of something else as he opened a tin of cigarettes.

The contractor sighed. 'How cold it is!'

After a moment, he told the tenuous man in the corner, 'Privacy or not, won't they be cold? We could have asked them to come in.'

'They wouldn't have even if we had.'

The doctor smiled and said, 'Then perhaps in the newlyweds' honour we could...'

'Leave the waiting room to them?' The slim book lover stood up. Slight and wiry while also firm and workman-like, darting about like a bird with shy but restless eyes, he didn't seem to look directly at other people. Without another word he walked up to the door, then returned and sat down on the nearest available chair.

'I think we're worrying too much about the newly-weds,' observed the Delhi man, offering his tin of cigarettes to the others.

'No, thanks,' said the doctor.

The other three lit up, and for a while were sheathed in smoke. They started when the door was opened again. A uniformed bearer entered to ask if the gentlemen wanted anything; the refreshment room was closing.

With nods from the rest, the bureaucrat said, 'Coffee.'

Silence once more. All this while there had been sounds outside, people walking around, calling out. It hadn't been evident earlier, but as soon as the noise subsided everything seemed a little too quiet, unnaturally quiet for such a large station. Now the passengers had probably settled down for the night somewhere, wherever they could, however they could – those two had found a place too for sure, they wouldn't be visiting the waiting room again. The line was closed, no more trains would be arriving that night, no bells would ring. Whether it was the porters, the hawkers or the cigarette vendors, the bustle was over for now. And it was so very cold. In the dim light of their waiting room, these four people who didn't even know one another, the subtle blue smoke of their cigarettes their only companions, felt as though the world outside had been obliterated and they had found shelter on an unwelcoming, comfortless island. They no longer seemed unfamiliar to each other; in fact, there was even a feeling that all four of them were probably thinking the same thing. That couple, who had only given them a glimpse of themselves at the door before disappearing, had left something behind, as though the bird of youth had shed a few feathers as it flew by: some sign, some warmth, some pleasure, sorrow or tremor that refused to dissipate, something with which these four individuals – even if they did not speak, even if they only thought about it silently – would be able to survive this terrible night.

Suddenly the doctor said, 'Perhaps it was rude of us.'

'Still thinking of them?' the Delhi man laughed, but it was obvious from his manner that he hadn't forgotten them either.

'I was thinking – thinking of something else; I was wondering how long such days last for them.'

Now the Delhi man laughed out loud. 'Is that anything to wonder about? Don't we all know the answer?'

'Afterwards, all of us know it,' spoke the lean-faced book lover, 'but at the time none of us does. For instance, can those two even imagine how short-lived it all is? Can they imagine that they will not continue much longer exactly this way? That is the most amazing part of this amazing illusion.'

'Amazing illusion! Well put!' the contractor nodded his agreement.

The coffee arrived.

'Is everything an illusion then?' A shadow of concern seemed to descend on the contractor's enormous face.

'At least this coffee is no illusion. The smoke is palpable. Sugar for you?' The elegant doctor busied himself, pouring out the coffee.

The contractor's keen curiosity appeared to have overcome any languor; he abandoned his easy chair and, pulling a chair close to the other two, putting his hand on the chilled table, he leaned forward and said to the book lover, 'Is everything an illusion then? Nothing remains? You're the writer – why don't you tell us?'

The man seemed embarrassed at this, having the title of writer bestowed upon him, but did not delay in his response.

'The memory remains. Ultimately only the memory remains, nothing else.'

'What's the value of the memory?'

'None!' the Delhi man announced cheerfully.

'Eats into work, wastes time, makes you sad. Come, let's have our coffee.'

Still the contractor persisted: 'Is the memory of happiness that has passed, happy or sad?

A mocking smile emerged on the lips of the man from Delhi. 'No point thinking about that, but if you'd tell us a story, the time would be well spent.'

'Story! Story of what?'

'I mean – we're all old men here, there are no ladies, so speaking openly will not be indecent, will it?'

'What are you getting at?' The fat contractor seemed apprehensive.

'He's saying,' the doctor explained, 'we had our days too, like the ones that couple has now…'

'I didn't,' the contractor protested, and immediately his five-o'clock-shadow-marked cheek reddened in unseemly mortification.

'You too,' said the writer. 'There's no one who has never liked someone. What happened afterwards is not the point, that liking is what counts. Maybe it's memory, too, that counts. Some kind of memory…'

'I haven't any,' the contractor protested loudly, waving his hand. 'I'll listen to your stories instead.'

'Fine, we'll tell our stories too,' the doctor said solemnly, looking at his large, discomfited co-passenger. 'But so must you. There's no hope of sleep tonight, let's listen to stories through the night. Let's start.'

'Are you talking to me?' About to lift his coffee cup up to his lips, the contractor paused.

'I'm a businessman, I don't understand anything but business, things like that…'

'Yes, you too have your story,' the writer spoke confidently.

The contractor was silent, his head bowed, for a while. Then he said, 'I don't have a story, but I know someone else's – a friend's…'

'Fine, let's hear his story.'

The contractor took a sip of coffee and began.

Chapter Two
Makhanlal's Sad Tale

Let's call him Makhanlal. As the name suggests, he was an ordinary, average kind of fellow, but he was held in high esteem at home. For he was the first college graduate in his family. His grandfather had had seven sons, those seven sons had borne another thirty-two, and who knew how many more those thirty-two had produced – it hadn't quite ended yet. But not one of these tall and able specimens of masculinity had got past that barrier of school yet; some had tried and tripped. There was no end to Hiranmayee's – Makhanlal's mother's – unhappiness about this; she needled her plump husband Raghab so much about this, at every opportunity, that the man couldn't say a word in retaliation. Both of her elder brothers had BA degrees, she herself had read up to class nine at the Nilfamari Girls' High School. So the day her first child – and first son – Makhanlal had been born, she had vowed to ensure that he earned a BA.

Fulfilling her pledge hadn't been easy. The atmosphere at home was imbued with the somnolence of the orthodox landowning classes. For generations it had not occurred to anyone that they might have to work for a living, so no one was too concerned with drinking from the font of learning. And while their affluence had certainly diminished, the attitude had prevailed; the menfolk still lazed their way through the day, bathing at two in the afternoon, luxuriously eating their luncheon off plates surrounded by several bowls of delicacies, and then happily, serenely, embracing their bolsters in readiness for their naps. This siesta was a family tradition, and they had not abandoned it despite their having become paupers. The dearth of money certainly hurt, but the pain of earning it was even more intense.

Hiranmayee's Raghab spent his days in this way, and would have continued to do so, had Hiranmayee not vowed that her son would earn a college degree. Languishing at the family residence in the country wouldn't do, it just wouldn't. So as soon as Makhanlal passed his school examinations at the village school, she goaded her husband into moving to Calcutta.

As agreeing was the easiest option, Raghab acquiesced; in the process, he gradually had to give up his aristocratic habit of indolence. Soon after arriving in Calcutta, he liquidated some capital to set up a small shop in Bhabanipur. Needless to say, this too was at his wife's advice. Hiranmayee had finally convinced him that they wouldn't be able to keep body and soul together much longer if they kept reliving the memories of their landowning days. Investing her brains and her jewellery, which was of course her husband's capital, she provided him with a business to run.

It soon became a thriving carpentry shop; Raghab was interested in woodwork, and had even built some furniture with his own hands. So although he started reluctantly, gradually his work became his passion. The one thing he couldn't give up was his siesta, but barring those two or three hours, the rest of his day was spent at the shop. The goddess of wealth looked upon him favourably because of this diligence, and her favour made him even more hard-working. Within a couple of years, a new establishment was born: the South Calcutta Furnishing House.

Raghab had wanted Makhanlal to get involved with the running of the shop from the beginning: to immerse himself, learn the ways of the trade, become familiar with the smell, the touch, the colours of wood. As the work-load increased with the growth of his business, he was increasingly eager for his eldest son to begin helping him. Wasn't the intermediate degree enough – why go further? What good would a college degree do? The business star was in ascendance; if this good fortune wasn't made use of right now, what if it gave them the slip? Wasted logic! Even if everything was lost, Makhanlal had to get his degree.

The day they received news of Makhanlal's having passed that hallowed BA examination, you can imagine Hiranmayee's joy. Her dream of twenty-one years had finally come true. So pleased was she that her happiness gave birth to an impulsive proposal: she said, 'I want to get him married.'

Strange, isn't it? Does anyone believe, today, that a BA is the only qualification required for marriage? A mere college graduate, Makhanlal was no more than a boy. How could he get married!

But there was nothing strange about it as far as Hiranmayee was concerned. First, this was a family tradi-tion – not one of her uncles or her father had crossed eighteen without marrying. Even if you were modern when it came to education, you remained traditional where marriage was concerned. Theirs was an affluent household, and a bride would only make their cup of joy brim over. And the boy wasn't one of those typical, bespectacled midgets – just see how handsome he was.

Yes, he was indeed handsome – there was no denying this. I know – knew – Makhanlal very well; at twenty-one he was a burly, powerful giant who looked thirty-two. Large and ungainly, he had prominent teeth, a manly, hair-covered chest, enormous shoes that caused great consternation when they were sighted lying around. Seeing as he could easily pass for a father of three, it didn't seem suitable for him not to be married.

That too, the bride was at hand: Subhadra-babu was their next-door neighbour, and Hiranmayee had picked his daughter out a while ago. Was the reason her beauty or her father's wealth, you ask? Neither. Subhadra-babu was a semi-impoverished college professor, and the girl – I heard the details from Makhanlal – was not exactly what you would call beautiful. But the learning! The father was a scholar and Malati – the girl's name was Malati – was no less. Having earned three stars in her final school examinations, she was now in college, apparently glued to a book even during her meals. And what an assortment of books all over their house, my God, had anyone ever seen the like of it? It could be said without the slightest exaggeration that Hiranmayee had never seen so many books with anyone in her own family, that was for certain. It was at her husband's ancestral home that the fewest books could be found; there was no reading habit there. Her Makhanlal followed in this mould; whether he had a college degree or not, he never turned the page of a book. Their family was truly peculiar.

Perhaps the idea of choosing a bride on the basis of her collection of books sounds unusual, but as you've probably realised this was where Hiranmayee's weakness lay. If the family disposition was to change, a bride from a scholarly family was essential – this was Hiranmayee's reasoning. In other words, just as she had attracted the goddess of wealth through the bait of wood, now she wanted to use the lure of a bookish daughter-in-law to attract the goddess of learning. Their backgrounds were beautifully compatible – why not get it over with in July, she decided, November was still a long way off.

Laying out an elaborate meal for her husband, she broached the subject. Raghab was amenable but had a different line of thought: a big fat dowry would enable him to expand his business. Hiranmayee dismissed the idea at once, saying, 'If destiny wills, the money will come on its own – why should you have to beg for it?'

'No, no, it's not a question of begging, just that... Avinash-babu was saying the other day...'

'Who's Avinash-babu?'

'His shop is next-door to mine.'

'The liquor shop? Ugh – a wine seller's daughter?'

'Not exactly a wine seller, his background is different. Seems interested, too. Maybe you could take a look at the girl – it would make sense all round...'

'Enough. I'm the one who's done all the thinking for you – don't get in the way now.'

'As you please. But will a professor's son-in-law still be interested in running a shop?'

'Is that what's worrying you? My Makhan isn't like that. I can promise you he will take over the responsibility for our family very soon.' Hiranmayee turned to her son. 'Well? I hope you agree?'

Makhanlal had been eating next to his father – he paused at this question. He said nothing, only looked very solemn, lowered his face and started to trace patterns on his plate. The answer was obvious, you could see as much; shoulders that were broad enough to support the entire family were not going to find it troublesome to bear the responsibility of a slender young woman.

Are you wondering whether there's a history to this? Yes, there is. Mother Nature never spares us from her wiles – be he so powerfully built, even his broad, hair-covered chest cannot prevent a tiny flower from budding within.

The thing is, Makhan ran into Malati virtually every day. 'Ran into' is perhaps the wrong way of putting it; he could see her every day. Their neighbours' inner veranda was visible from his room, and there was hardly a day when a light breeze clad in a sari didn't lead Makhanlal's mind to wander. Of course, like a true gentleman – or perhaps in embarrassment – he averted his eyes immediately, though not without stealing a glance or two. Sometimes Malati would bring a cane chair with her to the veranda. She seemed supremely oblivious to the fact that someone close by was watching her, or could be watching her – she sat there and read, laughed, spoke loudly, hummed songs with her brothers and sisters. Everyone knew you weren't supposed to stare at a lady, but if the lady chose to present herself before you all the time, you weren't expected to gouge out your own eyes, were you? Many a time Makhanlal was not even aware of what he was gazing at, but the moment Malati left the veranda for her room, he realised why his eyes had been roving. And was it just the eyes? Had the heart beneath his wide breast not been beating faster too?

This was the history. Hardly anything – and yet, was it entirely insignificant? Makhanlal, you've guessed correctly, was a bit of a simpleton; unlike the quick-witted city boys, he had not acquired a great deal of the knowledge of certain subjects they had learnt at an early age, precocious fellows. He was happy to be able to see Malati, indeed he felt as though he really knew her. Did he know that in Malati's universe her well-built neighbour did not even exist? Did he think about it? Maybe he did, maybe he didn't, but when he did think of her, it wasn't as anyone other than an intimate. Hence he was not very surprised at his mother's proposal – nor was he overjoyed, accepting it as inevitable. He even drafted out in his mind that first night in bed, how he would talk to her; how he would conduct himself with the occupant of the next-door veranda when she became occupant of his life. His first question would be: did you ever see me from your veranda? What would her reply be?

A day or two later, Hiranmayee got down to business. After lunch she changed into a mint-fresh sari with a red border, marked the vermilion on her forehead so it was a little more prominent, popped a paan[2] into her mouth, and headed off to the professor's home. When she returned, her smile had been wiped out; nor was any other kind of pleasant expression displayed on that mouth which had earlier consumed paan so happily.

Raghab was home napping, as it was siesta time. But this day, his age-old habit was broken. From his room,

Makhanlal could hear only the sound of his mother's voice speaking continuously, occasionally interrupted by the sound of his father's soft comments – but every time she raised her voice, he could hear what she was saying.

'What? Shopkeeper! Shopkeeper's son! And what do they have to be so pompous about? Professor? And how much does he earn anyway? All our property, all those boats, all those celebrations – have they ever seen anything like that? No. They didn't even give me a hearing. "We're not thinking of her marriage yet, she's still a child!" Child indeed! How much more of a tomboy will they let her become? Like him? My son is as good as anyone else. Hasn't he got a college degree? Isn't he a good boy? Does he lack for food and clothing? Where will they find a more suitable boy? She's so dark, what prince will take her away on his golden steed? They were so fortunate that I... oh!'

It was the same story over and over again. Raghab probably fell asleep, and Makhanlal gave up trying to listen. But he could still hear his mother speaking, on into the afternoon, for quite a while longer.

Hiranmayee smarted under the insult for a few days. The added injury was that no matter how much she wanted to get her son married, she wanted even more to have Malati as his bride. 'I told them, "If you'd like Malati to continue studying, we'll take care of it, a daughter-in-law with a BA would be a matter of pride, we have no demands by way of dowry," but they didn't even entertain the idea. Oh my God, their arrogance. But why – may I know why? Is it because they eat their pathetic meals at a table?'

'Oh, please be quiet, ma!' Makhanlal protested in a low voice. 'The houses are so close to each other, what if someone hears?'

'Let them,' Hiranmayee moved towards the professor's veranda and raised her voice a few decibels more. 'Am I scared of them? Am I going to beg them for this? Huh, I have such a wonderfully eligible boy in my son, what do I have to worry about? Take my word for it, Makhan, a day will come when they will burst with envy when they look at you. I guarantee it.'

The storm continued thus for a few more days, then the topic of Makhanlal's marriage faded gradually. Avinash-babu, the liquor shop owner, got his daughter married off by July, many other virgin foreheads were touched by vermilion, but the subject of the marriage of Mr Makhanlal Ghosh, BA, and his special ability to shoulder the responsibility of a wife never even came up. Certainly there was no lack of unmarried girls in Bengal that year, but despite all her talk Hiranmayee just didn't take the initiative. Why not? Couldn't she have got a wonderful bride for her son and astonished the professor's family? Would that not have been her natural response? Certainly. Just why she behaved to the contrary, I cannot say. Had she really imagined she would be able to wreak some kind of extraordinary revenge on that scholarly family? There was no indication this would ever be realised. A month went by, two months; not even out of a sense of courtesy, or even out of mere neighbourliness, did the professor's wife pay Hiranmayee and her family a visit, although Hiranmayee had visited them a few times now. The veranda remained as uncaring as before. There were still gusts of laughter, the flash of a sari, but Makhanlal no longer looked that way.

You think it was out of grief? No; Makhanlal possessed that singular virtue of not understanding grief or rejection. The truth was, he had no time. He woke in the morning, ate a frugal breakfast and went off to the shop, came home for lunch and took a brief rest, then went off to the shop again, only returning late in the evening. He had taken most of his father's responsibilities on his own broad shoulders. Practically all of them, actually. His enthusiasm was matched by his enterprise, and if he lacked for a brain in that great big head of his, he compensated for it with sheer hard work. I saw him back then, working like a horse, shuttling between different places in town. Where did he have the time to think of the talented daughter of the erudite professor?

No, he did not have the time for this. Only, he felt a little uncomfortable whenever he passed the professor's house on his way in and out of his own home. Suddenly he felt he was too tall, too fat; maybe his clothes were dirty, his gait and posture terrible. The professor's drawing room was on the ground floor, by the road – try as he might, Makhanlal could not resist stealing a glance every once in a while. Did he see anything? Nothing, only a blurred hint of something behind the curtains. Sometimes the curtains would part by chance, and then he could see… an unknown world. In the house Makhanlal had known since birth, everything was unkempt; even clean meant half-dirty. But here was a well-decorated room, in it a gracious welcome: paintings on the walls, rows of books. A different world altogether. Laughter, snatches of conversation, perhaps the flash of a sari. Some days it would so happen that Makhanlal's feet refused to move, at that moment. The heart within his muscular chest beat a little faster; suddenly the carpentry shop, that hand-run printing, all felt as dry as wood, as anaemic as paper. But whenever he felt that way, he lengthened his stride, ran to catch his tram, and forgot everything in the rush of work.

It was the middle of the second year of the Second World War. There was a feast of money in the interiors of the supply office, you could smell it in the air. Like many others, Makhanlal headed towards it – maybe a little apprehensively, but the returns were undoubtedly beyond his wildest expectations. It helped that he looked older than his years; maybe his powerful frame evoked trust, or perhaps he had more staying power. Whatever the reason, he succeeded in getting a lot of quick orders through contacts and persuasion. And then when Japan joined the war in winter, it simply – but all of you know what happened…

It was an amazing time. There were no people in Calcutta, you couldn't add another person to Calcutta, Calcutta bombed, thousands of people dying on the pavements. The two-paise stuff cost twelve annas; neither rice nor sugar, coal nor salt was to be found; all you could get was khaki, jobs and a bounty of cheap cash. It seems amazing to think about it now, and it seemed as amazing back then to Makhanlal. Perhaps it was destiny – or was it his mother's blessings? – but anything he touched seemed to trigger an avalanche of money. A bounty of cheap cash was to be made by supplying material to the armed forces. He used to get practically a porter's load of cash, he couldn't fit it into his pocket; the notes were bundled up in newspapers and deposited in the bank. Every day he'd deposit more money, write out fat cheques, and somehow the days, weeks, months and years went by. He had lost track of day and night when one morning he discovered he had become a millionaire. Really.

Where there used to be a small shop in a lane, there was now a huge factory, a showroom on the main road. Makhanlal was now the provenance of a hundred people's bread and butter. Both his younger brothers quit college to join him at work, and this time Hiranmayee raised no objections. As for Raghab, he was now retired, retired on full pay! His landowner's spirit soared and thrived on the vast current of his son's accomplishments; every morning he would buy enormous quantities of food for the day's meals, then gossip with his wife, sitting on the doorstep of the kitchen, have a leisurely lunch, spend the afternoon sleeping and, sometimes, discuss the accounts in detail with Makhanlal at night. Since his son had taken on the responsibility of earning, he had returned to the respons-ibility of spending. Of both spending and not spending, actually – in other words, how much to spend, how to spend it, how much to save. Raghab was involved in re-solving these complex issues, and Hiranmayee's approval of his participation in their financial planning was so assured that Makhanlal didn't have to do anything at all in this respect. He didn't have the time, nor the inclina-tion; brimming over with the impulse of the work itself, he was actually relieved to leave everything to them. Food and clothes were plentiful now – the food even more than the clothes – but even when food prices were going through the roof how much could you eat, and the burden of having a lot of money caused no less worry than the anxiety of not having enough. Appearances remained unchanged, however, still stamped with the untidiness of poverty: no one would have realised that the family's earnings had not just doubled or quadrupled, but grown tenfold.

You think it was self-discipline? Not exactly, though perhaps they had not indulged in small luxuries, preserving their riches for large-scale displays of affluence. For securities held their faith! Raghab kept buying up land, not to mention Hiranmayee's gold and jewellery purchases. Soon, it was time to arrange the daughters' marriages. Very soon for the elder one, if traditional norms were to be applied, though as for the younger girl, Hiranmayee's second vow was to get her through college as well. She would be the mother of not just a son with a BA degree, but also a daughter with a BA degree. 'Let them see, let them realise we're no less when it comes to academics.'

Them, of course, referred to the next-door neighbours, and mostly to the vain wife of the professor. Learnt your lesson? If only you had agreed to the marriage, your daughter would have lived like a queen, my son's a millionaire now.

Hiranmayee had been going so far as to send news of their good fortune obliquely, through the shared domestic help; she didn't forget to inform them once. Certainly not on the day Raghab purchased a half-finished house in Ballygunge. Her messages reached their recipients, but the professor's family never broke their silence. Their obliviousness to their neighbours equalled Hiranmayee's inability to forget about hers. Strange was her competitiveness, extraordinary her desire for vengeance.

It was now said that the professor's household could no longer afford meals. Perhaps this is what happens when the gods smile on you; even Hiranmayee's desire to lay waste to her neighbours' self-sufficiency was almost fulfilled. Very pleased to hear this, she recounted the story to her son in great detail.

It was certainly a story to be recounted. The professor had apparently not received his salary for six months; his obscure college had never paid salaries properly. They'd pay eighty and extract a receipt for two-fifty. So never mind the airs and graces now, the professor's family was actually bankrupt. He'd survived on private tuitions and writing guidebooks. Now that there was a shortage of paper, nobody was publishing guidebooks anymore, and with everyone getting jobs left, right and centre, who needed a private tutor? Apparently things had come to such a pass that...

Having listened silently till this point, Makhanlal asked, 'How did you get to know all this?'

'Well, Harimati does the dishes at their home too. Yesterday she was saying she can't continue there – after all, these poor people all do this work for a living, if they don't get paid... Never mind servants, apparently they don't even get provisions every day – and the girl is supposed to take her BA exams this year, the fees have to be paid...'

Here the dutiful son Makhanlal may have said something to the effect of, why discuss other people's affairs;

maybe he made an even softer protest. Hiranmayee changed her tune immediately, 'You're right, of course, what business is it of mine – just that I was thinking of the girl, she couldn't get married and now she can't take her exams, so what I'm saying is, enough of educational lessons, if you agree I can organise a different kind of lesson!'

Thick-headed Makhanlal was unable to read between the lines of this subtle proposition, so she elaborated.

'Should I sound out the professor's wife? I'm sure they'll be gratified if we so much as throw a bone their way!'

Her face suffused with a victorious smile, she looked at her son; but Makhanlal's normally grave face looked almost stern, and he left without saying a word, only muttering 'Ridiculous!' under his breath as he left. It wasn't entirely clear who the comment was intended for.

He was late getting home that night. As he passed the professor's house he suddenly remembered what his mother had said. Pausing, he raised his head to look at the house. Dark – except for a light in a first-floor room where a fan whirred, its huge, dark shadow moving around the wall at regular intervals. This was all that could be seen – nothing else. His mother was probably wrong on all counts, they seemed just fine. At least, this was what Makhanlal tried to believe. But how much could you make out looking into a first-floor window from the street?

A small thorn embedded itself in Makhanlal's breast. It would prick him every now and then. Were the neighbours really in such a bad way? No, no, all this was his mother's imagination! She loved to think they were in trouble, she was troubled by needless envy – so she exaggerated and made up stuff. But what if she were right? She could be, couldn't she? But what business was it of his, what could he do, what was there for him to do – nothing, nothing. There was nothing for him to do, even if next door they were – assuming his mother was right – short of food and clothing; he would not be able to do anything despite his largesse, which exceeded all needs or expectations. His thoughts pained Makhanlal in a strange way and made him angry with himself – am I like my mother, am I not able to forget about them either?

Meanwhile the turmoil of the war continued, day after day, month after month. It seemed the war wouldn't end during this lifetime. But where was the hurry: how many times did people get the opportunity to make money, especially Bengalis! And meanwhile, Raghab plunged himself heart and soul into the Ballygunge house: raw material was bought at controlled prices, and the contractor assured him that the work would be completed in four months. The ungainly appearance of their home, the lack of striking furniture – Hiranmayee wanted revenge thrice over for all of this too. Therefore, brand new beds, tables, chairs and wardrobes, made to measure according to the dimensions of each of the rooms, were being built at their own factory. Makhanlal bought teak at sky-high prices, and poached craftsmen from Park Street, pledging double wages. Yes, Makhanlal joined his parents' enthusiasm, their 'conspiracy' against what they had been – not exactly out of choice, what option did he have? The good thing was that his workload increased. Come hither, O work! You're the saviour for the hapless soul who has nothing else in his life, who has gathered no riches of the mind.

Makhanlal was now in such a state that he was relieved only when he had pushed through the train of actions and thoughts that made up the day to the deep sleep of midnight. All he wanted from the day was that it should go by. Some days would pass without a bath or a meal – he neither noticed not cared.

But Hiranmayee noticed, and rebuked her son in a suitably affectionate manner. How long would his health last like this, how could someone who needed to move around so much not get himself a car. Hadn't Tarapada down the street spoken of a car...

'Couldn't get it, ma.'

'Hah! Not get it once you've decided you want it?'

'Never mind, I'm doing all right without.'

'This is a terrible habit of yours, get others all they want, but be a miser when it comes to yourself. How can people take those crowded buses these days!'

'Everyone does, ma! Even girls.'

'Girls! Don't talk to me about girls. They're not girls anymore – every last one of them has become male. Bags slung across their shoulders, they're a sight, each of them. Oh, by the way, the professor's daughter has got her BA and found herself a job. The father is going to live off his daughter now.'

As soon as this subject came up, Makhanlal sidled away, and started shaving before the mirror. But Hiranmayee followed him and said, almost to herself, 'How does it feel? It's hurting now – oh, if only I'd agreed to her marriage then – if only I'd known – so why not come out and say it?' Hiranmayee inevitably found her way back to the same issue over and over again. A few days later,

Makhanlal was on his way back from Dum Dum in a taxi when he stopped at a red light by the governor's residence. It was nearly evening, closing time at offices; even looking at the buses made you afraid. Three or four girls stood on the pavement, on their way home from office. How could they take a tram – would they even be able to? Why worry about all this, they did it every day, they were used to it. But Makhanlal glanced at them again. This time it seemed – perhaps it had earlier too – one of the faces was familiar. Yes, it was she – the professor's daughter. The taxi had stopped close to the kerb and Makhanlal could see her clearly; he had never seen her so close. Malati was looking at the road hopelessly. Her face wore the gracefulness of fatigue: weariness seemed to suit her beautifully. Makhanlal glanced at her, then at the empty space on the seat beside him – twice or thrice her glance came his way, but never once did their eyes meet. Should he call her? But how would he address her? And would... would it be right? What if she was offended, what if she said... What if she said nothing... But... While he vacillated, the red light turned to green, the taxi started moving; that hopeless anticipation Malati and those other girls had, of taking a tram, was left behind.

Makhanlal had been headed home, but he suddenly changed his route and went off to Chitpur, to pick out a mirror for their dressing table, for their new home.

Several months went by.

Raghab had almost finished building the house, the furniture was ready; all that remained was an auspicious day to move in. Hiranmayee was busy inspecting every-thing they owned, selling off useless stuff, trading in old saris for aluminium utensils, distributing worn out clothes to the needy. There were all these ancient trunks from her father-in-law's time, the paint had worn off, some of the locks had broken, but they were very strong. One morning she was wondering what to do with them, when her youngest daughter Lakshmi ran up and told her the police had surrounded their neighbour's house.

'What?'

'Yes, ma, the police – and lots of people. Come and take a look!'

Lakshmi tugged at her mother's hand, but this was unnecessary. This was, after all, something everyone had to witness, not just children but also adults. Especially Hiranmayee.

Her first stop was at her veranda facing the road. There was a small crowd outside the professor's house, and the policemen's red headgear was glittering in the sun. The downstairs door was wide open – it appeared to have been smashed in from the outside; some people rushed in, while another man hammered at the professor's brass name-plate and took it off the wall, throwing it on the road. Hiranmayee looked on, hypnotised. Four porters brought out the professor's yellow upholstered sofa and put it on the pavement; then came the chairs, then the centre table... Passers-by stopped in their tracks; the balconies and windows of all the nearby houses bore eyes that blazed with curiosity and fearful amusement, perhaps accompanied by a little pity.

Hiranmayee's gaze moved to the veranda inside the professor's house. From here you could see their veranda too, and images of daily life, hear floating snatches of laughter, of music, of the tinkling of the joys of life, all of them oblivious to the neighbours' existence.

That veranda was now empty and silent. The doors and windows were shut, there didn't appear to be anyone inside. Harimati had revealed everything to her: the professor's family owed months and months of rent, and the landlord had now asked for their belongings to be confiscated by the court.

Everything would be dragged away. And then? Would they be dragged out on the roads too – the professor, his wife, their two young children and that office-going, graduate daughter? Would the professor be handcuffed in full view of everyone and taken away? Oh dear – really? Poor fellow, how sad, what a scene!

'What a scene!' Hiranmayee ran off to tell Makhanlal. 'They handcuffed the professor and took him away.'

'What!'

Calculations of wood, steel, nails and bolts swirling in his head, Makhanlal was preparing to go to office when Hiranmayee flew in and gave him details of what had happened.

Makhanlal was late leaving for work that day. What he thought when he heard the news, what he felt, I have no idea. As for what happened afterwards, I will recount it the way I heard it from him, with my imagination filling in the gaps. By then, he discovered as he went out to the veranda, many more of the neighbours' possessions had been pulled out onto the pavement: bookcases stuffed with books, the dining table, a radio, a gramophone, large, framed paintings. Makhanlal took one look and returned to his room. Hiranmayee arrived to continue her litany: 'Oh dear, how sad for them, but then how will our worrying about it help, it was fate, and then again, why call it fate if you don't keep your spending within your limits' – but Makhanlal neither responded to any of this nor looked his mother in the eye. 'It's very odd,' she continued, 'There isn't a trace of anyone at home, have they run away? But then they've been living in the neighbourhood for so long, they must be embarrassed to be seen...' Et cetera, et cetera. When none of this could get her son to break his silence, Hiranmayee asked, hoping for an answer, 'Aren't you going out today?'

Makhanlal said, 'Hm,' but kept sitting. So Hiranmayee had no choice but to go away, returning to the veranda to continue observing the goings-on. By then it had all become stale. The fresh excitement of the morning had vanished; the curious eyes had disappeared from nearby balconies; the busy morning was underway. Everyone was in a rush to get to work, to get the cooking done; staring with your mouth open at someone else's affairs wouldn't get you to office, and how long could you gape anyway. Besides, this would obviously take a lot more time to wrap up. On the pavement, under the sun, lay the professor's impotent furniture – the bed with bedclothes still in place, his writing desk, cups and saucers, the electric fan. More was on its way, households didn't survive on just a handful of things. Hiranmayee decided not to tarry any longer, asking Lakshmi to man the observation post and going off to the kitchen to supervise the cooking.

When sympathetic neighbours went back to their own lives, when curiosity was buried under sizzling sounds from kitchens, when the buzz around these sensational events had almost been reduced to the level of daily mundanity, this was when a door in the house opened and a girl emerged – the same girl whose fluttering sari on the next-door veranda had touched thick-skinned Makhanlal once. He hadn't set eyes on her for a long time now, but that day, sitting in his room, Makhanlal saw her, seemed to recognise her, definitely recognised her. He leant on the railing for a bit, raised his hand to sweep his hair off his forehead, and then suddenly returned to his room, the door shut again. What he did then was a little strange, perhaps you will laugh at it. Why he did what he did was something even he didn't know, but at that moment, he told me later, it 'came upon him', everything seemed to happen on its own.

Makhanlal refused to delay any longer, slipping his feet hurriedly into his sandals. His ungainly frame emerged onto the street. The heap of furniture on the pavement had almost reached their own home, and the varnish on it was glittering in the eleven o'clock sun. He wended his way through all of it and stood before the house next door. The wide open door posed no obstacle before him, and discovering the staircase – without hesitation or doubt – he went directly upstairs. The drawing room was like a new widow, only a picture hung on the wall, like a blood red memory of a long life. In the next room a few blackened, perspiring labourers were tugging at the family's belongings; Makhanlal went past them in long strides. There was just the one more room, in the corner, its door closed. Was the family in there? He knocked on the door – no response. Another knock, and then a light push on the door got it to swing open; the scene inside no longer remained hidden from his eyes.

It was a small room. There was nothing in it except the four white walls, though the marks on the floor where the furniture had stood had not yet been erased. Huddled on the floor were the inhabitants of the house: the professor, his wife and daughter, and the other two children curled up on the floor, asleep, one's legs on the other's body. Having seen these people only from a distance, suddenly seeing them up close in these unusual conditions jolted Makhanlal into realising how distant, how remote they actually were. Why was he here? What could he do?

They were silent, too. The professor raised his eyes only to lower them immediately, and his wife didn't raise hers at all. The only one who stood up, briskly, was Malati – of course Makhanlal hadn't forgotten her name, all these months.

She came to the door quickly and said, 'You? Why are you here?'

Her tone was rough, without a trace of welcome in it, and yet Makhanlal heard music. 'You? Why are you here?' could only mean that she had recognised him, that she knew who he was. His uncertainty fell away, boldness suffused his soul. He spoke without effort, 'I had to come. Something needs to be done.'

Malati was probably about to say something, to utter some protest born of strong self-respect, but Makhanlal left immediately. The landlord's people were on hand, and he spoke to them and resolved everything within the hour. The professor joined them, speaking in a feeble voice, even objecting as much as he could in the circumstances to Makhanlal's intervention. Eventually, when everything was settled, when those same perspiring labourers returned everything to its place and proceeded to arrange things properly, then – by then – the professor was so exhausted he couldn't even utter conventional words of gratitude, for which Makhanlal was extremely thankful.

The rest of the day passed in flight for him. How lovely the day seemed, his work, the people, Calcutta – possibly he loved the entire world that day. And the kindness of the world too seemed limitless; whatever he asked for was being granted with one word, there seemed to be no obstacles at all, anything he wished for seemed to materialise before him instantly. His journey back home after his day's work was different too. Every day, he returned because he had to, because even exhaustion set its limit – but that day it felt as though someone or something was awaiting his return. The night and the breeze seemed to suggest as much.

His feet slowed down naturally before the professor's house. The rooms were lit up, the shadows of the fan blades were whirling as usual on the first-floor wall. Surely everything was fine, there could not have been any other problems, but still, he thought, let me check. Was it pure philanthropy? Didn't he have an ulterior motive? Just as this question occurs to you now, it occurred to someone else too. And that is where this story ended.

As soon as he knocked softly, the downstairs door opened, and it was Malati who Makhanlal saw standing before him. He would have been happier had it been someone else, but it was too late to retreat now.

'I just came…'

A completely unnecessary announcement, and when the person he'd addressed said nothing in response, even the dim-witted Makhanlal realised its redundancy.

'...find out if everything's all right...'

'Please come in.' She spoke like a doctor inviting a patient in. 'Yes, everything's all right.'

Makhanlal entered. When he looked around everything seemed fine: the pictures on the walls, the books on the shelves, the radio in the corner, all just as he had seen on his way to and fro past the house. Once upon a time he had imagined a lot of joy in this room, but now, in this beautifully arranged setting, his day-long happiness seemed to fizzle out; it appeared to have no basis, no meaning.

'Please take a seat.'

He didn't want to at all, but something seemed to compel Makhanlal.

Malati sat at a distance and said, 'I knew you'd come. I was waiting for you.'

Makhanlal felt a tremor run across his stout body at these words.

'There's something I want to ask you.'

'Yes?'

'Why did you do this? Don't be quiet, answer my question.'

Makhanlal looked into his interrogator's eyes and realised he had erred.

'Why did I do this? I have no idea.'

'You have no idea? Then let me tell you. The self-satisfaction of philanthropy is no mean thing. It feels wonderful to get a chance to help the poor. The gratitude of other people is delicious, isn't it?'

Every word tumbled out of this modern, educated woman's shapely lips with lucid articulation. On hearing so many obscure words at one go, thick-headed Makhanlal became even more stupid. He could say nothing in response.

'And besides, you have your own motive too. You decided that you would bring us under your control and take revenge on us.'

Makhanlal could hear nothing but meaningless sounds in words like 'motive' and 'revenge'. He groped for words, just as a person gropes in the darkness, but could find nothing to say, nothing that he' could say.

'But what you think will not happen, it can never happen.'

Now Makhanlal stood up and said, 'I thought nothing, maybe I have created difficulties for you, those difficulties... please forget them.'

'Only after your money's returned can we forget. But get it back you will. Maybe it will take time, but we will definitely return it.'

'All right.'

'Another thing. Do not come to this house again – never, not for anything.'

Makhanlal turned near the door and said softly, 'No, I will not come.'

Back on the road, Makhanlal walked past his house. He walked around for hours that night, with that awkward gait of his indecently proportioned body. The thoughtful darkness of the blackout was sympathetic, uninquisitive.

The room had been echoing with the contractor's deep baritone all this while. As soon as he stopped, night descended more heavily on the waiting room, attendant to its expectant silence. From afar, penetrating the veil of fog, came the sound of shunting, like a stifled moan during a dream, and from even further the sky was rent by the anguished cry of a dog. When the sounds died away, the Delhi man coughed mildly and said, 'Is that the end of your story?'

'Do you need to hear more?' a smile appeared on the edge of the writer's lips.

The senior bureaucrat, even used as he was to everyone's obsequiousness, was not thrown off his stride by that derisive smile. He asked gravely, 'Perhaps I may be pardoned for asking a question: did the professor return the money?'

The contractor reached out for a cigarette. His hand was like a claw, the knuckles extremely thick and covered with hair. His face was so large that the small cigarette hanging from his lips looked rather ill-fitting. Blowing smoke like an amateur, he said, 'This is all I know of Makhanlal's story, I do not know the rest.'

'There is no need to, either,' the veteran writer observed. 'What happened after that, whether he met the girl again, how she felt after insulting her benefactor, whether or not she used to pretend to read by the downstairs window in the hope of seeing once more that huge, ugly man – all this is irrelevant. The girl of our dreams, who lives in our heart, Makhanlal wanted to see her for one time as a real person – that is all that is real, all that matters, nothing else does. Surely Makhanlal would have married a girl of his mother's choice after they moved to their new house – by now he must have a full family of his own, children, he must be earning a lot too – but none of these subsequent events can cancel out the earlier one. Whatever Makhanlal had to get from his Malati, he has got already, he will never lose that, don't you think?' The writer looked at the contractor as he concluded.

'Never mind Makhanlal, it's the others' turn now,' the contractor showed his large teeth as he laughed.

'Your turn,' the doctor winked at the bureaucrat.

The man from Delhi seemed prepared. He didn't waste his time refusing – he had probably planned his own story while he had been listening to the previous one; probably the result of office discipline. Just as he did his work on time in his office, he started his story the same way, in a low, smooth voice, using small words...

Chapter Three
Gagan Baran's Tale

My name is Gagan Baran Chatterjee. I am a minor celebrity in Delhi and Simla, where they know me as G.B. Chatterjee. The initials G.B.C. have been scrawled on important government documents at least a thousand times. I went to England at twenty-one, and upon my return at twenty-four I got a job in Delhi. I've lived there ever since. So long have I been there that I can no longer imagine living, or ever having lived, anywhere else. After retirement? I've made arrangements for that too. I have a house at Civil Lines in Delhi, you can see the Yamuna from the veranda. Bengal's damp climate doesn't suit my wife's health – her father used to be the principal at Agra College. Our children speak in Hindi-laced Bengali, and they speak in English even more. Even this conversation with all of you in Bengali – this too is new for me. I hardly ever have these trysts with Bengal any more, I don't even feel any attraction. Once in a blue moon when I do go to Calcutta it's on official work, I don't stay a day longer than necessary.

And yet it was in Bengal that I was born, that I grew up, that the first chapter of my life was spent. Back then, in that distant childhood, could I ever have imagined myself as I am now? Nor, for that matter, can I now picture that boy, that shy young man, as the first edition of myself. All those memories seemed to have been wiped clean, I thought I had forgotten them all – but suddenly, after our conversation, it's all come back so clearly.

I remember a boy from an ordinary Bengali family, aged seventeen, studying at a small town college. Having won a scholarship for my matriculation results, I was at the centre of everyone's intense expectations; most of my time was spent trying to live up to those expectations. You may find it hard to believe now, but I really was an innocent back then, the quintessential 'good boy', ever obedient, a hard-working student, extremely courteous to all and sundry, to the point where I didn't even dare look them in the eye.

But so what? Within me, the spirit of seventeen was quietly doing its work. You spoke of love; I used to dream of it too. Learning the formulae of chemistry had taken so much effort, but the basic formulae of life were there to be learnt on their own; they advised trying to add colour to one's life, if temporary, and I was no exception to this. Countless were the number of novels I lapped up, in between textbooks, all the titles you get in our small town – yes, I even read – as a writer, you'll laugh. Even poetry. In poetry or in prose, wherever there was romance, there my heart got its sustenance – and how strange it was too, not all the writing in the world could alleviate my longing. The more I heard about it, the more I wanted it.

Today, I feel that no matter how much I heard about love through the written word, I heard nothing; even if I did, I did not listen. But when I heard it at seventeen, from Pakhi, melody flowed from flutes to fill the skies.

Yes, back at that distant age of seventeen, Pakhi had loved me. I can recollect her exact shape as I speak, she's coming to life before my eyes. Black eyes. It was in those eyes that love was born, in those eyes that love lived its life; in those extremely conservative times, there was no other language available to us. I would be present as others talked amongst themselves, and so would she – but I cannot remember our having said a single word to another then. Or perhaps that conversation of the eyes was a form of conversation, one that sated whatever hunger we felt then. At least, we harboured no hope of anything more, nor did we have the opportunity for it.

But this same Pakhi finally spoke one day, one night, on a winter night such as this one.

It was about three in the morning. Imagine a small town, the road cutting through an enormous field to one side, fog all over, and the pale radiance of a dented moon hanging in the sky. The play staged at the Railway Club had just ended – it was a major annual event – and every home was represented in the audience. The women were the eager ones, the majority of the men present merely escorts. That exalted post was mine for the night, despite my youth, simply by virtue of my being male. The elders were reluctant, while there I was jobless and without any examinations looming before me – entirely available in other words, which was why the womenfolk pinned me down. I wasn't very keen, but in those days it was simpler to do something, even unwillingly, than to refuse.

The women still sat behind a screen back then, but there had never been anything to block out their voices. Even if I could not see them, I could hear them, their giggling, their conversations, their bickering over seats, their observations about the play, their admonitions of their children; a mix of peculiar cries. There was plenty of shouting on stage too. As I nodded off sleepily, I felt I was watching two different plays, no, three – for since I was sitting close to the stage I could hear the prompting too, not to mention the fact that Draupadi and Bhimsen could be seen smoking on the side, occasionally. This three-piece din went on and on, showing no signs of relenting – I kept dropping off every now and then – but the play simply would not come to an end.

Finally, when it drew to a close and everyone pronounced it a grand success, the only regret we had was that as it was December, we could not carry on till dawn. Then it was time to go home. There was no transportation of any kind, people began to walk home in groups. For part of the way, everyone followed the same road. Everyone knew each other, so the noise emanating from the women continued non-stop, as though the play had not really ended and kept following them all. Suddenly the judge's car roared by and then – or so it seemed to me – it was silent all around, bitterly cold, field after field stretching in every direction beneath the dead glow of the moon. You could not tell the tree apart from its shadow, and even the people trudging along seemed to be their own shadows. In a while there was no one else nearby, I was walking alone. I realised I had left my female companions behind; I must have been walking quickly because of the cold, and enjoying the walk. Just a few minutes earlier, I had been on the verge of sleep, but now I felt not a trace of it – in that enormous open field, on that foggy night, I felt every molecule in my body telling me I was awake, I was alive.

But had I pressed too far ahead? Was I neglecting my duty? Of course, having a boy who had just acquired a baritone and a moustache beside them was not likely to be very helpful; on the contrary it would be inconvenient. But still, what if I was needed?

Pausing for breath, I looked behind me. The women's group lay far behind, barely visible in the fog. But it seemed someone was walking swiftly towards me. Who was it? A girl. Definitely a rebuke from my mother, or an order from my sister-in-law.

When she came closer, I saw it was Pakhi.

'What's the matter?' I said.

'Why should anything be the matter?' she replied.

'Well then?'

'What do you mean?'

'What brings you here?'

'They walk too slowly!'

I remember being surprised. What boldness! 'Did you tell them?' I asked.

'I did.'

'What did they say?'

'What do you suppose?' Pakhi shook her head impatiently. I looked at her with new eyes in the faint moonlight.

'Which means...'

Pakhi interrupted me and said, 'Are we just going to stand here?'

It was my first conversation with her. Suddenly I felt fulfilled, as though something heavy and profound had made its home within me.

We walked on, now side by side. But no more words the rest of the way. I walked swiftly, and not once did Pakhi say 'Slower'; she kept pace with me. She was fourteen then, quite grown-up by the standards of the times, rather placid too, by those same standards. But she appeared anything but gentle then; it felt as though her legs could carry her thus for ages, alongside me, beyond the houses, beyond the town, possibly beyond our small, familiar world to somewhere unknown.

So many thoughts crowd your mind in your naive youth. And why should they not? By then we had left the paved district road for the walking trail winding through the fields, slightly heavy of breath, burrs pricking our feet at every step – they felt like naughty caresses – and the smell of the grass, the dew, the earth all around. We walked thus for some time as in a dream, then the fields ended, the town narrowed into neighbourhoods; by the sleep-laden homes suddenly a pond appeared that had stolen the moon. Another bend in the road and there was the single-storeyed house Pakhi lived in. Our houses were next to each other, the families were close friends – everyone was friends back then, everyone was happy. That's the worst thing about the age we are at now, where it seems all happiness lies in the past.

Glancing back, I saw no sign of our guardians. We stood there silently as though in the wee hours of a winter morning, just when it's coldest, a spring breeze was blowing, breathing heavily, our bodies warm from the long walk.

A little later I said, 'You'd better get home.'

'In a while.'

I liked this idea. But though all this while I hadn't worried about a thing, here in this familiar neighbourhood, before this familiar house, I remembered our guardians. Maybe I had erred, maybe I deserved to be admonished, I should wait here with Pakhi to accept their rebukes humbly. Then Pakhi spoke. 'If only our homes had been even further... mmm?'

I said, 'But eventually the road would have ended.'

Pakhi glanced at me, her eyes glistening in the moonlight. Looking away, she said, 'What were you thinking of all this while?'

'I don't know.'

'I was thinking – I was thinking, this walk is lovely, but it's because we're walking on it that the road will end.'

Back then, I found this funny. But now it seems that fourteen-year-old girl had, without knowing it, spoken wisely. Our existence is like that: living eats into our life, all the roads we love end because we take them.

'I was thinking of other things too,' Pakhi spoke again.

'But I won't tell you, you'll laugh.'

'Tell me,' I gave her permission, as it were, drawing on all the maturity of my college-going self.

'No, I can't.'

'Why not?'

'I've forgotten.'

'So soon?'

'That's what happens to me. There are so many things I mean to tell you, but when it's time, it all slips away.'

'It all slips away?'

'Yes. I love you, that's why this happens. I forget it all.'

I trembled at her words. I looked away, so as not to have to look at her. The other womenfolk appeared at the head of the road. I was relieved. Who knew what else Pakhi might say? Were we scolded for having walked on ahead? I cannot remember. The others said something, but I didn't hear a word of it. My hearing had no room for anything other than Pakhi's parting words to me. I couldn't sleep that night.

Gagan Baran paused. The other three were motionless. There was no way to tell whether they had been listening or not: the contractor had turned up his overcoat collar to cover his ears, the doctor was wrapped in his blanket from the waist downwards, eyes heavy with sleep. The writer was leaning back in his chair, facing upwards, a cigarette burning away in his fingers; that he was awake became clear when he raised his hand to his lips. But this Delhi bureaucrat did not look at his listeners, studying the wall before him carefully, as though the rest of his story was written on it. The invisible writing of the past – which one cannot forget even when one thinks one has – swam up before his eyes, and he resumed in his smooth, slow cadence.

I remember another day. This time too, it was night, not day. This too was a moonlit night, but instead of winter's fog swept moonlight, it was a mad summer's full moon night. I lived in Calcutta then, it was the second year of my M.Sc. My elder brother had moved to Calcutta the previous year, and I had left my hostel to move in with him at his Shyambazar home. It was there that Pakhi had come to stay the night, en route to her new husband in Kurseong. Hers had been a big wedding. Devoting myself to mathematics had made me much less of a romantic and I was struck less by novels than I'd been before, but I felt it wouldn't be fitting not to have even a small feeling of heartbreak at Pakhi's having got married. I even managed to snarl at her in my mind, picturing her as having be-trayed me, but to tell the truth I felt no pain, no anger. Despite the stuff from the books, my heart remained intact. I was actually disappointed in myself, I went down in my own self-esteem, and, as far as I know, Pakhi hadn't breathed a single sigh either as she married the freshly minted deputy magistrate.

You may be wondering why she should have had cause to sigh at all. All this is part and parcel of adolescence, it cures itself with age, whoever frets about it afterwards? Yes, certainly I was being childish; as long as there were children in this world, that particular quality could not be purged. No matter what we say now that we're old, you cannot dismiss it. It's true, neither of us had thought of marriage, there was no scope for it beyond the relationship we had then, that was what we had accepted in our hearts. But did that mean it was to be classified as weak, poor, watered down? If that were so, why did I suddenly think so intensely of Pakhi now, all these years later in this strange place, at this strange hour? She had no lack of relatives in Calcutta, but she chose to stop at our house. I never asked myself why. My brother's wife loved her very much and she loved everyone in our family, even if there were a larger reason, a different, more real reason, I did not have the courage to acknowledge it.

No, I had not the courage. Pakhi arrived in the evening, I merely caught a glimpse of her. 'How are you?' are the only words we exchanged. Thereafter she became the property of everyone else, especially the women, for there is no creature more interesting to other women than one who has just got married, be she seven or seventy-seven. Late in the evening, everyone settled down on the veranda under the moonlight to chat, while I slipped away to meet my friends at their hostel. We used to meet often like this, but I remember how special that evening was, each of the friends like soulmates that evening. They agreed unanimously that they had never seen me in such good spirits either. Spirits? I don't know what name to give that feeling. Joy? Yes, it was a heartbeat, accelerating, fear-inducing, extraordinary kind of joy. Just as the miser cannot put his jewels out of his mind, deriving joy from the certainty that he has them, hidden away, so too was I joyous at possessing this – except that the miser fears losing it, while I feared seeing it, getting it, owning it. This was why my heart beat faster all the way back home, in pleasure, in hope, in apprehension, in happiness.

That moonlit summer night was truly wondrous.

I went to my room after dinner. The women congregated on the veranda again, outside. I sat and listened to their voices, their laughter, Pakhi laughing in her soft voice. As the night advanced, conversation flagged. I sat before my table lamp, a thick book open before me. I was really reading it, or trying to, even turning the pages occasionally, but what I read, or even what book it was, was something I remembered absolutely nothing of the next morning.

Meanwhile, over by the kitchen, the servants fell silent and the session on the veranda finally broke up. I sat on, listening to them shuffling around, to the small sounds of doors being locked. The noise on the road had died down too; the night was silent. I sat there, still, with my book open. Suddenly I saw Pakhi standing by my desk. The moment I saw her, I realised this was what I had been waiting up for. Yes, no point trying to hide it. I felt I had made her appear with the force of my longing – she had no choice, she could not have done otherwise. So I was not surprised, I said nothing, I only looked at her in silence. What was she like, the Pakhi I saw that night? That slim girl of fourteen, and this glowing young married woman – could the two even be compared? Tonight she was dressed in a blue silk sari, bedecked with jewellery of all kinds. I never could stand the sight of jewellery, but that night, that night it didn't look bad at all; it did suit some people sometimes.

Pakhi was the first to speak. I remember her words clearly.

'I'm a lady. You should stand up when you see me.'

I stood up obediently.

'Reading so late in the night?'

I glanced at the fat, open book in response.

'Are you up only to read?'

My head lowered itself in guilt. There was a silent pause. I could hear the ticking of the clock in the next room. There was one more sound, probably a sound in my heart, a strange one.

Pakhi spoke again, 'You're going abroad soon?'

'Planning to.'

'How long will you be there?'

'At least two years, maybe longer.'

'When will you leave?'

'In September.'

We exchanged only these words as we stood there, and then silence descended again. Several times I felt the urge to look at her, directly, face to face, properly, but I don't know what shyness prevented me. I kept my face averted though I knew in my heart, with all my heart, that she was there, near me, so near. But soon she wouldn't be.

Suddenly Pakhi came around and stood in front of me. 'Listen,' she said.

I raised my face to look at her. Her expression was severe, almost stern. I could see the rise and fall of her breath in the hollow of her throat; it was so silent all around, and she was so close, that I could practically hear the sound of that breath.

'You must do great things in life.' All of a sudden, I heard Pakhi's voice. 'Don't stay up any longer – you might fall ill. Go to bed, I'd better leave.'

I think I tried to say something, but not a sound emerged from my throat.

'I'll switch the light off before I go.'

I saw her hand touch my table lamp, and in a moment I was transported to another world. A dark, bluish moonlight came to life, my room was a room no more. Her blue sari looked almost black, and as soon as she moved her eyes glistened, her lips were painted by the brush of the lunar glow. I saw her for a moment like this, and then her long, strong, soft yet firm arms wrapped themselves around me; she held me hard and kissed me on the lips again and again. My eyes closed, my breath stopped, I felt the foretaste of death.

Then she moved away and said, 'I cannot give you anything more.'

She spoke and left. That night, too, I could not sleep.

Gagan Baran paused again. He tried to pour coffee into his cup, only to be disappointed: there wasn't any left, whatever there was had been drunk long ago. He lit a cigarette – he had probably been thirsting for one –

inhaled deeply, filling his lungs, and then blew the smoke out slowly.

The writer shifted and said, 'And then?'

Gagan Baran seemed startled to hear the sounds of another person, perhaps a shade embarrassed. What misguided notion had led him to start this tale? Never mind – what did it matter, after all? He was not going to meet any of them again. He tried to return to his present reality; he tried to think of Delhi, his job, his wife, his children, but none of them seemed very important at the moment, his head was filled with the echoes of the events he had been recounting all this while.

Transferring his cigarette to his left hand, he resumed.

Then I went abroad, came back: employment, marriage, children, promotions at work, getting older in spite of oneself. In other words, just like millions of others, my life too was proceeding on its pre-set, banal orbit. Yes, no matter how much you take care of yourself, live healthy, eat healthy, run to the doctor and the dentist, when it's time you have to get older, no one is exempted. My hair had greyed too, though you can't see it at first glance, but how long can you hide it. And I admit with shame that I see nothing to be proud of in having grey hair – I consider those who can leave this earth before they have gone grey fortunate.

There would have been no harm in not meeting Pakhi again, it would have suited this story better had I not. But that romantic chapter was far from my mind when I ran into her, which I kept doing, several times, at intervals of a few years. Each of those encounters was trite, abridged. She kept getting plumper; she loved her paan a little too much; she was perpetually cheerful, very happy, completely immersed in her children and household. I saw her daughter too once: she was growing up, suddenly she seemed to be her mother, the way her mother used to be as a child, all those years ago.

It was at this daughter's wedding that I saw her last – about three years ago. The wedding was in Calcutta, at Madhu Roy Lane. She had sent me a printed invitation card, to my Delhi address, along with a couple of handwritten lines to my wife: 'My dear, how happy I'd be if you could somehow make it.' She had met my wife a couple of times. My wife is a convent-educated woman, she found Pakhi rather rustic, but Pakhi had found an opportunity to tell me, 'Oh, you're a fortunate husband.'

It was just at that time that I had to visit Calcutta on official work. Debating whether to attend the wedding or not, I finally decided to go. Calcutta had long become a foreign land to me; I would visit for a day or two, stay at a hotel, spend evenings at the movies, never meet anyone but government officials. This time there was something else to do, somewhere else to go besides Writers' Building. The thought was not unpleasant. I had remembered the date, and thought I would go early and finish the thing off before the rest of the invitees turned up. I didn't have a dhoti[3] to wear, it was no longer a part of my wardrobe, so I went in my less suitable western garb.

It took quite some time to locate Madhu Roy Lane in Bhawanipur. Calcutta had changed a lot, and I seemed to have lost my bearings. Carrying a Benarasi sari[4] as a

54

present, I arrived at the wedding venue after evening had set in. Lights, decorations, shehnais,[5] overdressed young women and men, the faint smell of food being fried – I was confronted by this utterly Indian environment after ages. Just as I was feeling hesitant, as though I didn't belong there, a young man I didn't know welcomed me in, saying, 'Please come in.'

I said, 'My name is so and so, I'm here from Delhi, if someone could just...'

In a few minutes, a boy of fifteen or so escorted me upstairs. Pakhi's son, I hazarded a guess.

Pakhi was genuinely surprised to see me, and seemed almost improperly pleased. After a few pleasantries I said, 'I can't stay long.'

'All right, all right, I'll make sure you don't get late.'

Pakhi deposited me by myself in one corner of a room and disappeared. But I wasn't alone for long; elders from another generation gathered around me, one by one. Old men, old women; some without hair, some with blurred vision. An entire lifetime seemed to have passed since I had met them last. One by one, they began to speak – they appeared a little inhibited, but I could clearly make out they were happy to see me after all these days. I was happy too. They had known me when I was young, when I was a child – how much longer would such people live? It would soon be the turn only of those who thought of me as an old man, or an older person, or, at the most, a contemporary, to remember me. I forgot the weight of my years for some time, in this family gathering. I was surprised to see it wasn't difficult to converse with them. 'Where's he? How is she? What news of so-and-so?' These led to more memories, old memories, some amusing. I had never realised I remembered so much.

Pakhi appeared again after a while. She was carrying an enormous plate, small bowls arranged on it in a semi-circle. Oh dear. 'I won't take no for an answer, you must eat,' she told me at once. The old men and women joined in and I ate almost like a bride, head lowered, taking small mouthfuls, ending up eating most of it.

I stayed much longer than I had meant to. I met the bride, heard praises sung to my gift, and countless children arrived from all directions to pay their respects. Eventually I felt that the wealth of kinship I had experienced in those two hours would comfortably last me a lifetime.

Then, when it was time for the groom to arrive, the entire household animated, the shehnai playing afresh, I took my leave. Pakhi walked with me to the door, a few people behind her. We probably exchanged some words like these standing at the door:

'Well, at least we met again.'

'Yes. Couldn't stay for the wedding, please don't mind.'

'You go back tomorrow?'

'Tomorrow.'

'Take this,' said Pakhi finally, handing me a biscuit tin.

'What is it? Seems quite heavy.'

'Some sweets for your wife and children. Remember to take them with you.'

'Of course I will. Calcutta's sweets are famous all over. Unmatched around the world. They'll be thrilled.'

'Why don't all of you come over to Calcutta for a holiday?'

'Yes, let's see… this job… all right, goodbye…

As soon as I turned to leave, I heard a comment – probably from a grandmother type. 'Oh, you've got grey hair!'

I was about to come up with a light-hearted riposte when Pakhi softly touched my shoulder and said, 'Yes, our Gagan Baran, he too has grey hair now.'

Casual words, a casual incident, but will I ever forget the way she said those words! Never! In those words, in that little touch of her hand, I realised clearly that evening that Pakhi still loved me – it was probably that one time only that I realised, fleetingly, what love is.

Out on the street, the strains of the shehnai made me melancholy.

'Nice story. Ve...ery nice,' the contractor said, sighing loudly.

The writer said: 'But the moral is clear. You got the one you lost and so on. Love is somewhere else, in the distance, even if maybe it's only a wish for love, only imagination – not real at all. Many people have propagated this point of view over the ages, I don't subscribe to it.'

'Look, I don't know of any points of view,' said the Delhi man. 'I don't think about such things either. Eat, drink and be merry. I have no other viewpoint.'

'We're unanimous about that,' the contractor smiled.

'But both of you told us sad stories,' the doctor smilingly quipped. 'How about a happy one now?'

'Of course, of course.'

'The story of my marriage. Barring those who die before their time, everyone – fine, maybe not everyone, but most people – eventually ends up marrying someone or other; there's nothing unusual about that. Still, there was something interesting about my marriage, it's not a bad story.'

'Never mind the modesty. Let's hear the story.'

The doctor began…

Chapter Four
Dr Abani's Marriage

I had been practising barely a year when I got married. I hadn't thought of getting married quite so young. Having got myself a chamber in Dharmatalla and a telephone connection, I even had a small car, but no clients to speak of. According to my calculations, the estate my late father had left for his only son would last five years or so – if I couldn't build a practice by then, shame on me.

I had decided not even to think of marriage until I was earning at least a thousand a year. All those people who got into their wedding finery the moment they got their sixty rupees a month jobs gave me palpitations. It's all very well to get married, but what about things like children, illnesses, the wife's whims, your own demands? And even if you managed to provide for all of these, there were the tiffs, the heartburn, the conflicts. All that was not for me. Or so I had thought. But things turned out differently.

The year I passed out of college my mother passed away, which meant I had no real family any more. Un-married young doctors normally tend to live slightly undisciplined lives; the person that I had become, who had no roots and didn't need to answer to anyone, it would have been easy to become debauched. But I succeeded in restraining myself – not through some extra-ordinary strength of character, but simply through my searing ambition to become a great doctor. After dinner, I'd study till midnight or one in the morning, and then, tired of medical textbooks, go to bed with a novel and resume reading the same novel in bed for a while, upon waking in the morning. This was my habit at that time, but it didn't last.

I laugh when I think about it now, but my heart beat with nervousness on the morning of my wedding day. I'd seen Bina in so many different situations for so long, spoken to her in public, and later in private, so many times, but every time I realised she was about to be my wife, that she would live in my house, sleep in my own bed, that her authority over my life would be more than mine – and that all this would continue not for a month or two, not even for a year or two, but all my life; every time this realisation hit home, I had no choice but to run and get myself a drink of water, or pace up and down my room.

Yes, I was very nervous that day. But I shouldn't be putting the cart before the horse. It's best to begin at the beginning.

I remember the first time I saw Bina. There I was, sitting in my patient-less chamber, dressed for the day, when my friend Ramen telephoned. 'Can you come over right away?'

'What's the matter?'

'There's this girl who's cut her foot – it's all swollen up – she's in a lot of pain…'

I laughed and replied, 'What do you want a personal visit from the doctor for? Put a boric compress on it, it'll heal.'

'No, it's just that – she needs to recover very soon, or else we can't get on with our rehearsals.'

'Rehearsals? For what?'

'You didn't know? We're putting on a play, *The New Nest*.'

I'd read a novel called *The New Nest* recently by Shailesh Dutta, who was quite a famous novelist back then. Was it being made into a play? The answer was yes. Dutta had written the play himself, and he was directing it himself too; the girl who had injured herself was his sister-in-law. She was playing the main role, but the poor girl could barely stand because of the pain, so I had to go over and cure her promptly. I was to go to Dutta's home. Ramen gave me an address on Lake Road; the lake was a new addition to Calcutta and Lake Road had been built very recently.

'What are you doing there?' I asked Ramen.

'I'm with them too.'

'Since when have you started hobnobbing with writers?'

'One has to keep in touch with everyone. Don't forget to come,' said Ramen and hung up. Ramen was a great friend of mine those days. He was a strange character; the first two years in medical college had convinced him he wasn't going to get through the examinations, so, dropping out, he opened an oculist's store on Free School Street. The shop soon moved to Chowringhee and an ophthalmologist with a foreign degree was installed, as was an Anglo-Indian girl at the counter. None of us had expected his business to thrive so much. We were a little surprised, to be honest; he didn't have much by way of physical capital. But he did have one divine form of capital – his appearance. You seldom found such a handsome Bengali; six feet tall, as fit as the centre forward of a football team, with a fair, ruddy complexion and a head full of curly black hair. It was his appearance, I felt, that was the key to his success.

These same good looks meant that the Anglo-Indian he'd hired as an assistant became so brazen that she didn't relent till she had married him. Friends like us tried our utmost to prevent it, but Ramen whistled his way to the registrar's office. Within a year the marriage was over, but Ramen couldn't care less. He ran his shop with the same enthusiasm as he had earlier and promptly hired another Anglo-Indian girl to run the counter.

Arriving at the Lake Road address, I found Ramen waiting for me on the pavement, pacing up and down. Getting out of the car, I said, 'At least we got to meet. We hardly see you these days.'

Ramen smiled in embarrassment, making the obligatory excuse. 'Been very busy. Come upstairs.'

Mr Dutta and his wife Gayatri both welcomed me with smiles. His book had charmed me earlier: I was even more charmed upon meeting him. Both of them seemed to be fine people.

After the greetings and formalities, I asked, 'Where's the patient?'

'Please come this way,' said Mrs Dutta, leading me into the next room. As all of you would have realised by now, the girl who was lying in that room was the one I eventually married.

She sat up apprehensively as we entered. I was amazed – could a mere cut on the foot cause a person to look as wretched as this? An ashen face, lips as dry as those of someone with high fever, reddened eyes, hair dishevelled and all over her face. A single glance told me the illness was a severe one.

And yet I could discover nothing, even after a prolonged examination. While I was bent over, checking on her foot, the patient sat still, chin on her knees; I straightened and asked, 'Is it hurting a lot?'

She didn't answer.

I asked again, 'Does it hurt a lot?'

Ramen said from my side, 'Answer him, Bina.'

The girl answered without looking at anyone, 'Yes, a lot.'

I wrote out an ordinary prescription, left the room and told the Duttas, 'It's hardly anything, and yet she seems to be in bad shape.'

Mr Dutta said gravely, 'Yes, in very bad shape.'

I spoke reassuringly, 'There's nothing to worry about. She'll be fine very soon.'

Ramen said, 'Small things sometimes flare up into complications, you see. That's why I called for you. I hope the play doesn't have to be called off.'

'No, no, there's no fear of that. She'll be fine,' I repeated, calming him down.

Whether it was because I was a doctor or for some other reason, both Mr Dutta and his wife seemed to have taken a liking to me. They invited me to attend the upcoming rehearsals; rehearsals were held thrice a week at their place. There was a rehearsal the very next day, so if I could make the time…

'I'll try my best,' I said, and took my leave for the moment. Ramen walked downstairs with me and said, 'I think you should come to the rehearsal tomorrow, you'll enjoy it.'

Now I usually spent my evenings in the company of friends – all of them doctors. Doctors never make friends with anyone but doctors. They don't like becoming friends with others, lest the number of free patients increases. But the same stories and jokes about the medical profession become boring after a while, and as I have mentioned I never participated in the exciting events young doctors organised to dispel that same boredom. So I couldn't dismiss this exciting new invitation. It was bound to be a different gathering there, definitely a novel experience. The next evening, amidst the bustle of Dharmatalla, as I wondered whether to go or not, Ramen marched in and instructed, 'Come along.'

'Where?'

'Aren't you going to the rehearsal?

'Are you?'

'I go every day.'

'Should I – really?'

'What do you mean, should you really? Of course! They'll be very happy.'

After dressing for civilised company, I got into Ramen's cream Morris. A little later, we entered Mr Dutta's drawing room. The concert of voices welcoming Ramen became restrained on seeing me. Many of them looked at me with an expression that said, and who on earth is this? Mr Dutta took charge of introductions immediately, announcing my name first and then, one by one, those of the others – no small labour, for at least twenty people were scattered around the room in small groups, some of whom it was rather difficult even to attract the attention of.

I hadn't guessed wrong. The taste of this gathering was completely different, I had not yet experienced anything in my life that I could compare it to. When had I ever seen such an assortment of so many beautiful, well-dressed young people in a well-lit room? Their laughter, conversation, bearing, brief glances around, even the slightest movement of their hands, all signalled that they were citizens of a brave, bright new world, one whose existence was not even suspected in the precincts of a medical college. At least that was my impression that day, though, as I got to know them better afterwards, I realised many of them were as ordinary as the rest of us. It was just that the polish on their casing gleamed more.

I had lost track of Ramen within a minute of entering. Everyone around us sought him out: sometimes with this group, sometimes with that, sometimes sitting, sometimes standing, sometimes half-inclined, he was laughing with his eyes, smiling with his mouth, speaking with both his mouth and his eyes. Ramen was fluid by nature, he had no inhibitions; anything he did seemed to suit him because of his fine appearance. I had always seen him become the toast of the party wherever he went, and here too he was the centre of attraction. Everyone seemed to have something to say to him in private, even. Mrs Dutta spoke to him in a low voice by the window for nearly ten minutes.

It appeared that Mr Dutta had been trying to get the rehearsal started for quite a while, but the conversation just didn't seem to cease. Meanwhile, cups of tea arrived, accompanied by elegant snacks. There wasn't enough for everyone the first time, though as I was a guest, I got some immediately. The second round didn't arrive till eight. Finally Mr Dutta stood up and said, 'Let's start now. We haven't done Anupam and Lalita's scene in quite some time, we'll start with that one. Anupam! Lalita!'

Ramen stood up and assumed a serious expression.

'Lalita! Bina, come on!'

The patient of the previous day had all this while been sitting quietly in one corner, leaning against the wall. I had noticed that she had not spoken to a single person in the crowd, not even looked up once. She had a book open on her lap, though her face made it clear she wasn't reading. Her face was as ashen as the day before. She had done her hair for the evening, changed her clothes, even applied a little make-up – but there seemed to be not a drop of spirit in her whole body. I had asked after her as soon as I entered, and Mrs Dutta had said she was better today. But I could see no sign of recovery. I admitted to a twinge of worry. A blood test might be needed, seeing how thin she was; even an x-ray was not a bad idea.

Mr Dutta called her again, 'Bina!'

Bina limped up on her bandaged foot. Mr Dutta said, 'Your lines, Ramen.'

I had not realised all this while that Ramen was acting too. And not any old role either – the role of the young lover I had read of, in the novel. I had enjoyed the romance between Anupam and Lalita the most, in the book. I settled down to watch closely.

Ramen was asking, 'Don't you recognise me?'

Bina said something unintelligible, softly. 'Speak up,' the author urged her from the back.

Now a faint voice could be heard, 'Anupam-babu, isn't it?'

'Look at him as you speak.' Bina raised her eyes with great difficulty and repeated her dialogue.

'Smile, smile as you speak.'

She smiled wanly. But there was no connection between the smile and her words, both seemed empty. I was wondering why they had chosen her for the role.

Mr Dutta stood up and began to lecture the girl. 'Bina, do you want all our hard work to go to waste just because of you? If you behave this way no one will be interested. Your role's the biggest, you have lines with everyone.'

Bina sighed and said, 'Leave me out.'

'What childishness is this,' Ramen smacked her lightly on the head. 'Stand up straight, say your lines properly.'

She seemed to tremble on hearing this, her eyes widened, blood rushed to her face. She didn't play her role half badly after that. And yet the lines of pain just didn't seem to leave her face; it was as though she didn't really want to say her lines, didn't even want to think them; she was just being forced to.

A little later Mr Dutta said, 'All right, let's do Act One now. Sarbeshwar, Basanti, Lily, Priyanath...'

Four or five people stood up to occupy the floor as he spoke.

The rehearsal went on till ten thirty at night. Many more friends, helpers and fans arrived: the room was full. The chairs had been pushed back against the wall and an enormous sheet spread out on the floor. I was seated on it in one corner, drinking it all in, watching, wondering and constantly being astonished. The people seated around me all looked talented or proficient in some way. One of them was indefatigably sketching the women present with a fountain pen; some were immersed, with their pencils, in calculating accounts, some were reading proofs. Occasionally three or four people repaired to the veranda, usually for private discussions; although their conversation didn't disturb the rehearsal, some of it reached my ears, as I was seated near the door. I felt a misfit in this bizarre dance, and yet I cannot claim not to have enjoyed it, for though I sat by myself I had no idea how time flew so quickly.

Around ten thirty, someone said, 'Let's call it a day.'

Mr Dutta said, 'Anupam and Lalita's last scene...'

Bina exclaimed, 'No, no, not that one.' I was surprised at the sudden vehemence in her voice.

Ramen said, 'Of course. Come, Bina, it's getting late.'

Bina rose slowly. She looked as though she wouldn't be able to utter a word, but how beautifully she played that last scene. When Anupam said, 'I'd better go, Lalita,' her eyes filled with tears as she said, 'No, don't go – don't leave me.' I was full of admiration for her performance.

Ramen was the last to take his leave, I had to wait for him. Mrs Dutta said, 'Do come sometimes, won't you?'

I nodded courteously, and Ramen quipped, 'Why sometimes? He'll come every day. He has no practice, you see, that chamber's just for appearances.'

Mrs Dutta smiled and said, 'Fine, why not set up your practice right here then? You are appointed medical officer of *The New Nest*.'

I said, 'That's wonderful, but I don't seem to have made much headway in my first case.'

'Bina? There's nothing wrong with her – she'll be fine soon.'

Ramen spent the night at my place. I used to work as well as live in my chamber, at that time. I ordered some fried rice and cutlets from the restaurant nearby, and we sat down to chat over coffee afterwards. 'Bina acts quite well,' I remarked.

Ramen smiled without responding.

'But she doesn't seem to be in good health.'

'Her health is fine, it's just been poorly of late.'

'It seemed to me her foot injury was nothing, there seems to be something else seriously wrong with her.'

'You're right there.'

Encouraged, I said, 'She's extraordinarily pale, I think it's anaemia. I could arrange for a thorough examination if you like. Perhaps Major Ghosh…'

'Do you really think a doctor can cure her illness?'

'What do you mean? Why not? you're half a doctor yourself – you shouldn't be saying such things.'

'But I know what's wrong with her.'

'You do?'

'Her illness is love.'

'What?'

'Love. What people refer to as falling in love. She's fallen in love.'

His words seemed to plunge me into water, from my safe refuge on land. I managed to compose myself in a minute and said, a suitably doctor-like expression on my face, 'I see. Then there's nothing that a doctor can do.'

'Not other doctors, perhaps, but you can,' said Ramen, bending his tall frame a little and lying down. 'Ah, this couch of ours is wonderful.' Rubbing one foot against the other, he continued, 'The thing is, the object of this girl's illness is me.'

I smiled. 'Not a new thing for you.'

Ramen suddenly became agitated. 'So what do you expect me to do? Die? Or leave the country? Bina's such a nice girl, I had never imagined she'd create such a terrible situation.'

Now Ramen started his litany of woes. How was he to get any peace if this kind of thing kept happening! He slaved at his business all day, the evenings at Mr Dutta's was a pleasant diversion, he had become intimate with them in a short time, they were very nice people too, or else it would have been impossible for him to show up there any more.

Having heard him thus far, I said, 'Well, I'm sure she's not the only one to blame – these things are never one-sided.'

'Believe it or not, it's completely one-sided. There's nothing from my side.'

'Nothing? Rubbish!'

'There you are, you're saying the same thing. I'm sure Mr and Mrs Dutta think so too. And as for me, I've exhausted myself trying to explain things to her these past few days. I can't take it any more.'

'What are you telling her?'

'I've been telling her to be calm, to be composed, to be good, to understand.'

'And what's she saying?'

'She can say nothing – she can only sob. I had no idea anyone could weep as much as she can. She's been transformed from a lively young woman into a corpse. And can you imagine how you feel when you see someone sobbing that way – especially when you know the tears are for you. The more I try to comfort her, the more wretchedly she sobs.'

The sum and substance of everything else Ramen continued to pour out to me was that he would have given up all contact with the family had it not been for the play. Besides, why should he give it all up? Did he not have a life of his own – his own happiness, his own peace? Should he stop visiting a place he wanted to visit simply because a young woman had lost her head? How unfair!

I consoled him with the thought that this was the tax he had to pay for his good looks.

Yes, he had realised long ago that his looks were his enemy. Just imagine, there he had been, enjoying his evenings at the rehearsals; and now tears threatened to drown it all. For the Bina I had seen, Ramen said, offered no hint of the kind of girl she really was. Bubbling, lively, pleasant – just the way Lalita's character was at the beginning of *The New Nest*. Mr Dutta might well have created Lalita in his sister-in-law's mould. Whenever she had come in through the door, the spectre of depression had flown out the window. A lovely girl, very nice, and if anyone had asked him, he would have vouched for the fact that anyone who married this sister-in-law of Mr Dutta's was a fortunate man.

'She has chosen the fortunate one on her own,' I teased him.

Ramen only sighed in response.

If only he hadn't joined the group. Everything had been fixed for the play, but they hadn't been able to find someone to play Anupam until they fortuitously discovered Ramen. Rehearsals went ahead full steam, for a month or so swimmingly. Everyone agreed that vivacious Bina was the last word where Lalita was concerned. They had known she would do well in the first part, where her character ran around all over the place and came across as altogether quite light and bubbly, but not even her sister had imagined she would play the romantic and sad scenes towards the end so beautifully. One day, however, everyone heard that Bina was very ill and would not be able to rehearse. Ramen got worried, everyone got worried, but they did not let anyone meet her – apparently she had a terrible headache and was lying down in a darkened room. The rehearsal didn't go off well that evening; Mr Dutta was distracted, Mrs Dutta kept disappearing inside every now and then, and finally the session broke up early. This was the point when Mrs Dutta took Ramen aside and said she had something important to discuss with him.

Ramen was thunderstruck at the news she gave him. Bina, Mrs Dutta reported, had been looking sullen yesterday, since afternoon, pacing from room to room, window to window. No rehearsal had been scheduled for that evening, and while Ramen sometimes visited even when there weren't any rehearsals, he hadn't that day. Mrs Dutta asked once or twice, 'What's the matter with you, Bina?' No reply.

When evening fell, the girl asked, 'Isn't Ramen coming today?'

'No idea – it's past eight, I doubt if he's coming today,' Mrs Dutta answered.

'Tell him to come – telephone him,' said Bina at once. Mrs Dutta looked at her sister in surprise and saw that her eyes were brimming with tears. No sooner did she exclaim, 'Bina! What's wrong?' and put her hand on her sister's shoulder, than Bina had put her arms around her and burst into tears, saying, 'I want to marry Ramen, I want to marry Ramen!' And so it had continued since then. Bina had given up on everything and retired to her bed. 'I'm in a spot,' Mrs Dutta had concluded.

Ramen had no idea what to say, where to look, where to put his hands in response. He felt terrible and yet, though he felt guilty, was it his fault? He had never said, done or even thought of anything that could have evoked such strong feelings in Bina. Mrs Dutta's account was difficult to comprehend.

He had no choice but to believe it when he saw her, however. She was in a wretched state. Ramen sat next to her and asked, 'What's the matter, Bina?' and apparently she immediately clutched his hand and started sobbing. She didn't even seem to remember how to properly conduct herself – had she gone mad? Ramen was flabbergasted, but also felt miserable.

The Duttas were incredibly courteous, and left the room. Ramen felt extremely self-conscious, and tried to overcome it with a laugh, saying, 'What is it?' There came a muffled reply. 'Hasn't didi told you everything?'

'She has.'

'What do you think?'

Ramen explained that they would have a lot of time to talk about this, but that right now she needed to recover so that the play wouldn't have to be abandoned; but his efforts were of no avail.

Now several days had passed, during which Ramen had tried in no small measure to appease the girl, to calm her, to persuade her to recover, with Bina's sister at it as well, around the clock – but no! They continued to flounder. For some reason Bina was certain that her life held no meaning unless she married Ramen, and no one could convince her otherwise. It made no difference to her that Ramen had been married earlier, and she particularly liked the fact that his lifestyle was a little westernised. Apparently this was the kind of man that was her ideal: tall, fair, someone who would climb the stairs whistling, play tennis, always be dressed in trousers. It seemed she had even told her sister that if the wedding didn't take place in normal course, she would move into Ramen's home – he wouldn't be able to throw her out, would he?

Ramen shared his litany of woes with me till two in the morning. Then he said, 'What do you think is the way out?'

Of course, I said, there was an easy way out; just marry her.

'You're asking me to marry her? If that were possible it would have been simple.'

'Why isn't it possible?'

Ramen said, 'I'm not exactly a fan of marriage.'

Now it was my turn to persuade him. 'Not fond of it? Meaning? You WILL marry, won't you? Surely you won't stay unmarried all your life? And there's nothing coming in the way either, you admitted yourself that you like her, you feel for her...'

'Why shouldn't I feel for her – I'm human too.'

'But then what's coming in the way of your marrying her?'

'Something IS coming in the way,' Ramen now made another confession. 'I've promised Ruth that if I do get married again, it will be to her.'

'Who on earth is Ruth?'

'Ruth is the girl in my shop…'

'Again, Ramen!'

'Can't you understand, she has no one of her own… And the way she's pursuing me – I'm very unlikely to get married again, but if I ever…'

I said angrily, 'So an Anglo-Indian's ploys matter more to you than a Bengali girl's tears?'

'Say what you will. I'm off to bed.'

Ramen yanked his jacket off and threw it on the floor, rolled his trousers up to the knees, and stretched himself out on the couch.

Enraged as I was, I said nothing more.

Sleep eluded me that night. I could see Bina's woebegone expression, puffy eyes, unkempt hair. I felt pain, and yet it wasn't quite pain, it was an unfamiliar pleasure. I imagined I was pacifying Bina, consoling her. She refused to listen, but I kept talking; once, she smiled, said something, and then I suddenly realised that Ramen and the girl who was so besotted by him were no more in my thoughts; I had forgotten about her. Embarrassing myself, I decided straightaway that getting involved in others' affairs was not wise. It didn't make any sense to visit the Duttas any-more, it was best to mind my own business.

But Ramen wouldn't let me be, he forced me to go along with him the next day. As I had said earlier, I enjoyed the atmosphere there. And in a few days I became addicted in any case; I stopped being a footnote to Ramen and started frequenting the place on my own. In that time Bina had finally got hold of herself, her face had acquired colour and a smile, she spoke beyond the dialogue she had begun delivering again, with such talent. With her recovery the pace of rehearsals rose; the intense level of socialising that went on before, after and during the rehearsals, was something I witnessed only at that one time, in my entire life.

In the first week of March, a couple of months after the first time I had been to Mr Dutta's house, in winter – possibly in January – *The New Nest* was staged. There were four performances. I was present on all four nights, sometimes observing audience reactions in the theatre, sometimes helping to arrange the actors' costumes before the enactment began, backstage. I wasn't spared the driving around to perform various chores, nor was I deprived of the honourable responsibility of dropping three members of the huge cast home post-performance.

The production came to an end, but the aftermath lasted another whole month. First at Mr Dutta's place, then at a restaurant, then at his friends' country home, and finally again at Mr Dutta's – feast after feast, celebration after celebration. Although I had not contributed much, having spent most of my time watching, I was invited to every celebration; the Duttas were flawless hosts. By now I'd had the opportunity to get to know several members of the troupe quite well, I no longer felt like a fish out of water amongst them. Although I was only a doctor, and far from well-versed in literary and related matters, several members of this glittering group had accepted me warmly. Of all of them, it was Bina I knew the least; no more than fit the tight confines of a formal relationship. I'd observed in her something of an antipathy for me. Maybe she didn't care for the way I looked, or perhaps she was aware that Ramen had told me everything about her – whatever the reason, she seemed to avoid my company. I did not mind this, for it was hard for me to fathom how to talk to, how to conduct myself with, a love-struck, love-singed young woman. This distance was far better.

In April, the Duttas went off to Kalimpong. I paid a visit the day they were leaving, and no one else was present except them, for a change. After some casual conversation, Mrs Dutta announced, 'Some news for you, your patient has recovered completely.'

Wonderful news, I thought to myself, but why tell me? My relationship with them was ending.

As though she had read my mind, Mrs Dutta said quietly, 'You know the whole story, after all, so I thought I'd let you know.'

After a pause, I responded, 'I do feel Ramen didn't do the right thing, in refusing to marry her.'

'He has given his word to someone else, there's no changing that.'

'Given his word? Rubbish. In truth, he doesn't want to get married.'

'Well, you can't force a person to go against his will either. I explained to Bina, "You can't have him, then why behave this way? Don't you have any self-respect? It's always the man who begs and pleads with the woman, and you, being the woman…"'

Mr Dutta quipped, 'Everything has been turned upside down these days, it's the women who do the pursuing and the men who do the running now. Poor Ramen. He wasn't in a position to be envied.'

Mrs Dutta said, 'Well, it was Ramen who managed to get things under control. I have to commend him, considering how taken she was, there would have been no escape for her had he been even remotely wicked.'

After heaping some more praise on Ramen, Mrs Dutta said, 'Now Bina says fine, let Ramen not marry her, but she's not going to marry anyone else either, not in her entire life. But we're going to be planning for her marriage soon. For now we're leaving her with my elder sister – you've met her, she was in charge of women's costumes for the play, and my mother's going to be visiting next month. She too will be relieved once the last of the brood is married off. Will you keep your eye open for a suitable boy?'

I nodded in consent, but her words seemed heartless. Bina had barely survived a major crisis – and to talk of marriage again so soon afterwards! Maybe what she had said was not entirely true, surely she wouldn't stay unmarried all her life, but it couldn't be easy for her to forget Ramen so easily. Not everyone could brush things away as easily as Ramen could!

Mrs Dutta said, 'My sister's house is on Southern Avenue, it would be lovely if you could visit them sometimes! They'll be delighted. And Bina's health, too – I'd really like it if she could live according to a doctor's regime for some time...'

'Certainly,' I said. 'I'll do my best.'

And thus began my visits to Southern Avenue. One or two people from the cast of *The New Nest* used to visit too, but most did not – the Duttas' home had been the destination of their pilgrimage; as soon as the Duttas left, the gathering broke up. And even if one ran into the others now and then, there was neither hide nor hair of

Ramen – he seemed to have been waiting for just such an opportunity; when the Duttas disappeared, so did he.

I put Bina through a round of calcium injections, pre-scribed two patent pills – one after meals and one before going to bed – and fixed a diet for her. The treatment appeared to be working; her cheeks grew redder, her eyes brighter, her skin silkier. Her eldest sister joked, 'Bina's blooming – marriage beckons.'

Her mother arrived from Benares, and the match-making began. But whenever a prospective groom was mentioned, Bina would fling her hands up, make a face and say, 'Oh, spare me, please.' By now the ice had thawed between us. Her mimicry of potential suitors, ranging from a young shawl-wearing professor to a widower landowner of Rangpur, accompanied by her comments, made me both laugh and feel sorry for those unknown gentlemen.

Her eldest sister scolded her. 'Bina, stop this tomfoolery. You don't seem to like any of them, you'll never find a husband this way.'

Bina said, 'Am I heartbroken because of that?'

Her sister retorted, 'Why should you be heartbroken. These days girls turn twenty-five, even thirty; still don't get married, they just go on being teachers till they're ready to drop. Let's hope it doesn't happen to you.'

'If that's what fate holds how can I avoid it?'

'Why are you being so unreasonable? Think of ma – she's getting on, how much longer…'

'We've been through all this, bordi⁶.'

'Why don't you tell us what kind of person you want – we'll look.'

Bina said, 'Are you telling me it's like an outfit or a shoe that you can order at a shop?'

All this was happening in my presence, I felt quite uncomfortable. Just as I was wondering if I could leave on a pretext, Bina's sister suddenly glanced at me and said, 'Why look anywhere else – you and Abani here are a perfect match.'

Bina went off in peals of laughter. 'What rubbish!'

Her laughter betrayed excellent health, but it didn't ring very nicely in this doctor's ears. I stood up and said grimly, 'Well, goodbye.'

Bina's sister said, 'You seem annoyed.'

'Not at all – I have some things to do, so…'

'Will you take us for a spin in your car? It's so hot, we'd love some fresh air.'

'Of course. Come along…'

'What about you, Bina?' asked her sister as she rose.

Bina came along too. After a couple of turns around the Dhakuria Lake, I stopped the car. Bina's sister wanted to sit on the grass, but as soon as we got out of the car she ran into a neighbour and the two of them walked on ahead.

'What would you like to do?' I asked Bina. 'Sit here, or catch up with them?'

Bina said, 'Might as well go back, this area has become terrible these days.'

'We'll go back when they return,' I persisted. 'Let's sit down for a while.'

The two of us sat down, and then there was no conversation. I was trying to dredge the shallows of my brain for something to say, when Bina suddenly said, 'My sisters imagine I've forgotten Ramen. But I haven't – and won't, either.'

I responded, 'I know. And I feel bad about what they say too.'

'But let me ask you something. Why do you hang about our place – aren't you supposed to be a friend of Ramen's?'

I cannot myself describe what my expression must have been like at that moment but it must have been quite terrible, for the moment she looked at me, Bina's expression changed as well. She said quickly in a low voice, 'Please don't mind, I shouldn't have said that.'

'You're right,' I said and stood up.

Bina stood up immediately too and said, 'I never say such things to anyone, I wish I knew why I said it to you. Please tell me you won't remember this.'

'But you're right.'

'No, I'm not. I'm wrong. You'll come tomorrow, won't you? Tell me you'll come.'

'I will.'

'Can you tell me something? Has Ramen married his Ruth?'

'I don't know.'

'Don't you run into him any more?'

'I haven't met him in ages.'

She didn't say anything else.

I said, 'If there's anything you want to tell him I can let him know.'

'No, I have nothing to tell him,' said Bina and sighed.

Her sister rejoined us. Bina rose and said, 'Let's go home.'

'So soon?' said her sister and looked at her, and then at me. 'What's the matter, have you two been quarrelling?'

Bina laughed in a manner designed to prove the complete falsity of her sister's surmise, but the laughter lacked authenticity. I didn't smile either.

That night I made up my mind. Enough, this was the end. If Bina could say to my face what she did, the mere suspicion of what she really thought made me break out in a sweat. The expression 'hang about' was eating away at my brain like termites. But it wasn't right to do anything drastic suddenly; that would be melodramatic, people would notice, it would become a topic of conversation. After all, I had developed something of an intimacy with these people over the past few months. Without revealing my intentions, I planned to gradually decrease the frequency of my visits, and then finally disappear – nobody would consider anything significant to have happened. I'd get peace of mind, they'd be relieved, Bina wouldn't have to put up with the unwanted company of a fool.

With this objective, I visited them the next day, to discover Bina all dressed up and waiting in the drawing room. She said, 'Ah, you're here.'

When I glanced at her she said, 'I was worried you wouldn't come any more.'

I realised this was a case of applying a balm of sweetness to the previous day's wound. Forcing a smile to my face, I said, 'Why shouldn't I?'

Bina laughed unaffectedly and said, 'That's what I thought. But how bordi scolded me last night!'

'Scolded you? Why?'

'It seems I'm very rude, unsocial, impertinent.'

'Why, what's the matter?'

'I've already admitted it was wrong of me to have said what I did – why drive it home further? Anyway, now that you've come, I'm relieved. Bordi, bordi…' Bina called out without getting up, 'Abani has come.'

I hadn't seen Bina in such great spirits recently – never, in fact – for from the time I had seen her, she had been overcome by love. She seemed like a different person, like a child, it was good.

After her bath, Bina's sister came into the room and said, 'Bina, could you get the tea please? They're making some snacks, get those as well.'

When Bina had left, her sister smiled at me and said, 'We've fixed her marriage with that court officer, Abani. The boy's family is in a hurry, and ma's getting anxious too. And really, how long can one delay these things?'

It seemed to me Bina was something of a burden to these people, that they'd be thankful to be rid of her. I didn't like the idea.

'We were thinking of next month – the twenty-ninth…'

'So soon?' the words escaped my mouth.

'We've written to Gayatri, they'll arrive soon.'

Things had progressed quite some way. And I knew nothing. Then again, why should I know – where did I stand in the scheme of things, after all? Was that why Bina was in such high spirits today?

Her sister said, 'What do you think?'

'I was only thinking…'

'Thinking what? That's what I want to know.'

'Has she agreed?'

'Bina? We can't afford to wait for her to agree. We can't all be as childish as she is, can we.'

So, she hadn't agreed? The marriage was against her wishes? And still so joyful? The tea arrived, so did the snacks, and so did Bina. But the tea tasted bitter, the snacks stale, I didn't even glance at Bina.

After I had finished my tea, Bina's sister said, 'Shall we go to the lake again?'

My mind was wandering, I came to with a start and said, 'Were you talking to me?'

'Of course I was talking to you. Let's not take the car, it's not very far, after all. A walk will be nice.'

She knew everyone in the neighbourhood; no sooner did we go out than she ran into someone she knew. A little later I noticed Bina and I had left them far behind. Back then, girls were just beginning to move around freely in that part of town. Observing this, I said, 'This freedom for women is a very good thing.'

Bina said, 'Do you think the freedom to move around freely is everything?'

'I think it'll grow to cover other things too.'

'I don't see it happening.'

The words had been on the tip of my tongue for quite some time, I took the opportunity to say them. 'Your sister gave me the good news.'

'What good news?'

'Apparently on the twenty-ninth of next month...'

'Are you mad?'

'You mean it isn't true?'

'Why don't you ask the one who told you?'

I didn't say anything more, but I felt much lighter. If I had had to hear from the same Bina who had told me the day before she'd never forget Ramen, that she was about to marry a young court officer of her own free will, wouldn't that have been sad? And yet, what was so sad about it – didn't such things happen all the time? Of course they did – every day – and what was wrong with it? And even if you could blame the others, there was no question of blaming Bina, for Ramen neither visited nor even enquired after her, he was probably immersed in Ruth, the scoundrel! If I could have, I would have forced him to marry Bina – but why was I so concerned, what responsibility did I have? Hadn't I vowed the previous night to put a full stop to this? Indeed, what on earth was I doing here, why did I even visit every day, why did I ever get involved with that play and the people in it? This was the time for me to expand my medical practice, I shouldn't have even been concerned with anything else. Suddenly it occurred to me that there would be no salvation unless I left Calcutta. Why not spend a few days in Darjeeling, and then get to work with fresh determination – yes, this was a good idea.

Engrossed in my thoughts, I suddenly heard Bina's voice, 'A penny for your thoughts.'

I replied immediately, 'I'm going to Darjeeling.'

It sounded discordant even to my own ears.

'Why?'

'Just like that – on a holiday.'

'When?'

'Early next month,' I said.

'Which means very soon…'

'Very soon…'

Bina suddenly stopped and said, 'Let's wait, they've fallen a long way behind.'

There it was. Since I was off to Darjeeling in a week, why break the routine for the remaining few days? My daily visits continued, and the promenade to the lake became a regular feature too. Bina's sister was the most enthusiastic about them, running into people from the neighbourhood every day and leaving us to chat with them. Bina and I walked a little, sat a little, sometimes speaking, sometimes silent. We discussed many issues those days by the lake, and, amazingly, discovered we thought alike on most of them.

On the first of June, Bina said, 'When are you going?'

'Going? Where?'

'So you're not going to Darjeeling?'

To hide my embarrassment I explained unnecessarily. 'Yes, of course I'm going – just that I'm attending to an important case right now, so…'

'You're definitely going?'

'Definitely.'

The more I said it the more my obstinacy grew – yes, I had to go.

Bina looked at the waters of the lake for a while and suddenly said, 'No, don't go.'

'Not go? What are you saying?' I could feel the tremor in my own voice.

'No, don't go,' Bina said again. 'You don't know – they've really – fixed everything… for the twenty-ninth – but I cannot – I cannot marry that court officer in trousers…'

Her description didn't make me smile, for I regularly dressed the same way, doctors had to. I said severely, 'Not everybody looks as good as Ramen in trousers, but that doesn't mean…'

Bina took the words out of my mouth, 'But that doesn't mean this idiotic character…'

I spoke like her guardian, 'Should such a thing be said about a respectable gentleman?'

'So, why doesn't the gentleman stay a gentleman? Take my word for it, none of what they're expecting will actually happen.'

'But surely you have to get married.'

'Why must I?'

'You're not a child – you know perfectly well…'

'You think so too!' said Bina, and gazed at the water again. I looked in turn at her eyes and at the water. They seemed similar to me; black and white, bright and moist.

Suddenly Bina turned to me and said, 'No – I cannot – you mustn't go – you must save me.'

'Me? How can I save you?'

As soon as I asked, I knew the question was meaningless; Bina had answered it long ago!

Ramen was the first to arrive on hearing the news. He leapt in the air, embraced me and spun me around, tipped the servants five rupees each – then left in a whirl and returned an hour later, in a whirl. Handing me an emerald ring and a sari with silverwork on it, he said, 'Here's your pre-wedding gift. Don't forget to visit the Duttas in the evening – they've just got back.'

Mr Dutta smiled when I met him. 'What's all this I hear?'

'So it really turned out to be the "new nest" for you,' said Mrs Dutta.

'So I see. The new nest for the new guest – it even rhymes,' joked Mr Dutta.

'Of course it'll match. The match that they've made will now ensure that.'

The couple continued in this vein for a while, and I laughed like a fool, red with embarrassment.

The days passed in a whirl. On the one side were the sharp verbal darts from the two future sisters-in-laws – here too Mr Dutta found a rhyme, pointing out that brave hearts attract verbal darts – while on the other was the business of finding a new house, buying things needed to set up home. Ramen went everywhere with me, arranging everything. I'd never have been able to do it all myself. And then – and then what else but that June twenty-ninth? I went to the new house. Ramen had been there since morning – he was the sole representative from the groom's side, and I still recall the exhilaration shining on his handsome face. Suddenly I felt a little sad too. It was he who had aroused Bina – and I was the one she had ended up with. Was I, then, just someone who was conveniently available? Had it been someone else at hand instead of me, would the outcome have been the same? Perhaps even that court officer in trousers? After our wedding, I had asked Bina about this and she replied, with that air particular to a bride, 'Uff!' Later, she added that she wanted to laugh when she thought about the scene she had created because of her infatuation with Ramen. Wanted to laugh? Already? On the chance that she had not married me, after a few months would she have – but it was ridiculous, why think of all these alternatives, life with Bina had turned out to be perfectly happy.

The doctor's testimony was received with excitement. The contractor might have been feeling drowsy earlier but as he heard the tale of *The New Nest* he laughed loudly several times, and even on the well-formed lips of the man from Delhi there appeared a faint line of amusement. Only the writer seemed lifeless, silent, with his hands in his pocket, his head lowered, but he was the first to speak when the doctor stopped.

'This was a matchmaking story, not a love story.'

'All right,' said the Delhi man. 'Now we'll hear the love story from you.'

'What time is it?'

'Nearly three.'

'Nearly three? How long the night is! How terribly cold! No news of our train yet?'

'None whatsoever'

'Then let's try for some sleep – even in our chairs won't be too bad.'

The contractor spoke in a voice hoarse from having been up all night. 'Nothing doing. You cannot escape. It's your turn now.'

The writer stood up abruptly, taking his hands out of his pockets and rubbing them together, then rapidly pacing around the room a few times. After this little show, he sat down again and said, ill-temperedly, 'Love story? When it's as cold as this? Fine, all right.'

Chapter Five
The Writer's Monologue

All three of us fell in love with her: Asit, Hitangshu and I. In the old Paltan area of Dhaka, back in 1927. The same Dhaka, the same Paltan, the same overcast morning.

The three of us lived in the same neighbourhood. The first house in the area was called Tara Kutir. Hitangshu's family lived in it; his father was a retired sub-judge who had made a lot of money, and built a huge house at the head of the main road. Tara Kutir was the number one house in the neighbourhood, in all senses: the first and the best. Gradually, many more houses sprouted on the land that used to be infested with grass and hidden thorns, but none of them could match up to Tara Kutir.

We arrived some years later, when the roof to Asit's family's house was being laid; Asit had arrived second, just before me. There was a time when ours were the only three houses in the old Paltan area; the rest of it was uneven ground, dust and mud, yellowish green frogs soaking in ankle-high monsoon water and plump, wet green grass. The same Dhaka, the same Paltan, the same overcast afternoon.

The three of us always stuck together, as much and as long as possible. Every morning Asit would wake me at dawn, calling 'Bikash, Bikash,' standing near the window at the head of my bed, and I would rise quickly and join him outside. Inevitably I'd see him waiting on his bicycle, one foot on the ground – he was so tall that my elbow hurt when I put my arm around his shoulder. Hitangshu didn't have to be summoned; he'd be waiting already by their small garden gate, or sitting on the low wall. Then Asit would ride off on the paved road to school, engineering school, while Hitangshu and I would roam around, hand in hand. The wind smelt of something, of someone, I can smell it still, I can remember something, someone.

Afternoons, the three of us would often go into town on two bicycles, sometimes for cutlets at Ghosh-babu's famous shop, sometimes to the only cinema hall in town, sometimes to the riverside with packets of peanuts. I never learnt how to ride a bicycle, despite my best efforts, but I took many a ride on those two-wheelers, a burden sometimes on Asit, sometimes on Hitangshu, on long journeys, standing or sitting behind them. Many evenings were spent in the fields of old Paltan, sitting or lying on our grass sofa, small stars piercing the sky, thorns piercing our clothes, the lantern on the front porch of Hitangshu's house piercing the dark and shining dimly, at a distance. Hitangshu couldn't spend much time with us in the evenings; he simply had to get back home by eight, as his family ordered. Neither Asit nor I were bound by such stern directives: we'd sit there in the darkness, call out to Hitangshu softly on our way back, and he'd interrupt his studies to covertly exchange a few words with us.

So the three of us were in love with one another, just as all three of us fell in love with someone else, back in Dhaka, back in old Paltan, back in 1927.

Her name was Antara. It was a rather sophisticated name for the Dhaka of those days. But nothing about her family suggested Dhaka, so why should their daughter's name smack of it? The gentleman was extremely westernised – or so we felt then – while the lady dressed in a way that made people mistake her for a young girl from behind. And as for her daughter, their daughter, what can I say about her? She strolled in the garden in the morning, sat with a book on the veranda after lunch, went for walks on the road in the evening; practically brushing past us, her voice could be heard at times – back in Dhaka, in ancient 1927, when it was not easy to even catch a glimpse of a girl, when a portion of a sari behind the closed doors of a carriage was a hint of heaven – and here was this girl, whom we would see in a different sari each day, and who was named Antara on top of that... We did not have the ability not to all fall in love with her.

But it was I who discovered her name. I had to sign for the bread every day, and one day I saw a new name in clear Bangla script on the bread-seller's register: Antara Dey. I looked at the register for a while, was possibly late in returning it, and then checked with Hitangshu in the evening, 'What's her name, Antara?'

'Whose...' But Hitangshu understood immediately and said, 'Possibly.'

Asit said, 'They call her Toru.'

Toru! There must have been at least two or three hundred Torus in Dhaka, but at that moment I felt, and I realised Asit felt too, that the language had no word sweeter than Toru. Hitangshu, of course, had to say something flippant and knowing, for the subject, or subjects, of our conversation were tenants of the ground floor of his grand house; unless he had more on the family than we did, he wouldn't be keeping his advantage over us. So he wrinkled his long nose and said, 'From Antara to Toru – I don't like it.'

'Why not, I like it very much,' I raised my voice, though my heart fell.

'If it was up to me, I'd have called her Antara.'

What audacity. What temerity! He'd have addressed her, and that too by her name! My face reddened with the heat of protest, and I was marshalling some sharp expressions in my mind, when Asit suddenly said, 'Me too.' Traitor! We would have these small quarrels quite frequently. There wasn't a day when we didn't talk about her, and there wasn't one conversation where the three of us were unanimous. She had been in a blue sari the other day, did she look better in it, or in the purple one? When she'd been walking in her garden that morning, was her hair in a ponytail or loose? The other evening, when she'd sat on the veranda with paper and pen, was she writing a letter or practising arithmetic? We would contend over such issues at the top of our voices. The biggest argument was over a strange topic: did her face resemble the Mona Lisa's a lot, slightly or not at all? I had just seen a print of the Mona Lisa and shown it to my friends; suddenly the words escaped from me one day: 'She looks a lot like Mona Lisa.' We had expended a lot of words on this thereafter without coming to a conclusion, but the good thing was that we started referring to her as Mona Lisa. No matter how much melody there was in Antara, how much sweetness in Toru, the three of us couldn't possibly refer to her by the same name everyone else used – coming by another name which nobody else but we knew, was almost like coming into possession of her.

We'd tell Hitangshu quite often, 'You're bound to get acquainted, it's the same house, after all,' and Hitangshu would blush at this suggestion of intimacy and say, 'What rubbish!' Which meant it could happen, and we used to speculate a lot about this, though we had accepted nevertheless that none of this would happen, that it was all talk, idle talk.

One evening, the three of us were on our way back from the Ramna river, me perched behind Hitangshu on his bicycle. We were chatting peacefully on that desolate path when Hitangshu suddenly stopped talking and wobbled on his bicycle; I was about to be thrown off, and trying to regain my balance I clutched at the collar of his shirt, which made him scream in pain, and finally I found my feet again. We heard a deep baritone just then, speaking in English, 'Take care, young men!' Mr Dey stood before us, we saw, along with his wife and daughter. Asit had his bicycle turned at an angle, his one foot on the ground, a heroic expression on his face.

'Really you must...' as Mr Dey spoke, his eyes set on Hitangshu. 'Oh, it's you. Keshab-babu's son!'

I watched as Hitangshu stared stupidly at his father's tenants.

'And them? I see the three of you together always. Friends, I assume? Wonderful. I like the company of young men, you must visit us some time.'

They continued on their way. We stepped off the road and lay down, side by side, flat on the grass. A little later, Asit said, 'What a to-do! Hitangshu got nervous, didn't he?'

'No, no, why should I be nervous? Just that the brakes...'

'Never happened before, and it had to happen now, just as we ran into them.'

'Fine. So what? I didn't hit anyone or fall over anyone. Just that I tried to brake suddenly...'

'No, no, you got off fine, only your face looked funny. And as for Bikash...'

I snarled as soon as my name was mentioned. 'Shut up. It isn't funny.'

'I think she smiled a little,' Asit still didn't relent. (There's no need to explain who he was referring to.)

'I give a damn if she did,' shouted Hitangshu, but the shout was more like a sob.

'Did you see, Bikash? Was it like the Mona Lisa's smile?'

'Don't make fun of what you don't understand.' My voice broke. I couldn't sleep well that night, remained half-dead for two days more and heartbroken for seven.

Still, setting aside our collective chagrin, Asit was undoubtedly the street-smart one amongst us. He kept saying, 'Why don't we pay them a visit?'

'Are you out of your mind?'

'Why? Mr Dey asked us, didn't he?' Eventually even Hitangshu and I came to agree that Mr Dey had indeed asked us to visit, practically invited us; he would be extremely pleased to see us, not visiting would be tantamount to showing disrespect. We became increasingly concerned with preserving his status. Every morning we would decide 'Today', every afternoon we would say, 'Not today.' Sometimes we saw them in their garden, on cane chairs; sometimes we saw a car parked outside their gate and realised that Mr Das, the only barrister in town, was visiting them; sometimes we concluded from the lack of visible activity that they weren't home. Once in a while we saw Mr Dey alone in his garden, reading the newspaper.

These seemed like opportune moments but our feet stopped moving just as we approached their garden gate, Asit's not as much as Hitangshu's, Hitangshu's not as much as mine; a little nudging and whispering, and eventually we walked past Tara Kutir, towards the main road. Most of the time we felt our visit would annoy them, and immediately we'd argue, why be annoyed, and why were we hesitating so much, didn't people visit people! We were neither thieves nor scoundrels, all we'd do was visit, take a seat, make conversation, leave – that was it!

It was an overcast day, with a slight drizzle. They seemed to be home. Asit was the first to enter after pushing open the tiny gate: tall, fair, handsome. Then came Hitangshu, serious, bespectacled, gentlemanly. And behind them, the diminutive me. We crossed the garden to the front porch, wondering if we should call out, what we should say, and so on, when Mr Dey himself pushed aside the curtain and joined us on the veranda. Clamping his teeth down on his thick pipe, he grunted, 'Yes?'

Even vivacious Asit was taken aback at being addressed in this manner. 'I… we… we dropped by – you'd said…'

Mr Dey recognised us in the fading light. 'Oh, it's you. Well…'

Asit said again, 'You had asked us to visit.'

'Oh yes, yes, of course…' he coughed and continued, 'come in, come in, all of you'; parting the curtain, he stood aside to let us through, but we just stood there.

'In you go.'

Trying to enter, Hitangshu tripped on the doorstep of his own house and trod on my toe. It hurt terribly, but what could I do but keep quiet! Dirtying the shiny

97

floor with our muddy shoes, we stepped forward. What a beautifully done up room, we had never seen anything like it. A Petromax light was burning. Mrs Dey was seated on a sofa in front, knitting, and further inside, on a chair pushed up against the wall, was our Mona Lisa, her eyes on an enormous blue book on her lap.

Mr Dey said, 'Sumi, these are the three musketeers of old Paltan. This is Keshab-babu's son, and these...'

Hitangshu introduced us. 'This is Asit, and this is... Bikash.'

Mrs Dey smiled and said, 'Are the three of you friends? How nice. We see you every day. Do sit down.'

We threw ourselves down on a long sofa, side by side. Mrs Dey called, 'Toru.'

Mona Lisa raised her eyes. 'These are our neighbours – and this is my daughter.'

Mona Lisa put her book down and rose, standing like a slender green sapling, swaying like a plant does in a slight breeze, bowed her head slightly, and then sat down again to lower her eyes to her book.

I thought I was dreaming.

Asit was from Calcutta, much smarter than the rest of us, much more in the know; and as for Hitangshu, he too had been to different places with his father, pronounced his words clearly and with confidence, and besides, his family owned Tara Kutir. Whatever little conversation there was came from the two of them; I was silent, staring at the floor, not daring to say anything lest my rustic accent was betrayed. The desire to raise my eyes for just a glance of Mona Lisa was eating away at me, but I just could not do it.

After covering topics like how intolerable life was without electricity, how dreadful the mosquitoes in Dhaka were, Mrs Dey asked, 'Do all of you go to college?'

Asit gave the appropriate answer proudly: 'Hitangshu has won a scholarship of fifteen rupees for his school examinations.'

'That's wonderful. My daughter is so scared of mathematics she doesn't want to take her exams.'

Suddenly a voice rose from the corner. 'Baba, how old was Keats when he died?'

Mr Dey looked at us and said, 'Do any of you know?'

Asit blurted out, 'Bikash does – he's a poet.'

'Really?' Mrs Dey put on a childlike smile and, for a moment – I sensed – even Mona Lisa glanced at me. My palms started sweating. There was a buzzing in my ear.

How long did we stay? Fifteen minutes? Twenty minutes? But when we emerged I was more tired than I was after five or six lectures at college.

Mrs Dey had forced an umbrella into our hands, but we didn't open the umbrella, we got wet in the thin drizzle as we disappeared in the darkness of the field. Suddenly Asit said – he never could stay quiet – 'Such wonderful people.'

Hitangshu immediately said, 'Really wonderful.' I didn't say anything, I didn't want a conversation.

A little later Asit said, 'You tripped again, Hitangshu.'

'When?'

'As you were about to enter.'

'Of course not.'

'What do you mean, of course not. And by the way, did you greet Mrs Dey when we entered?'

'Of course.'

Hitangshu paused and said, 'But when... Mona Lisa stood up to say hello...'

We exchanged glances in the dark, and even in the dark it was clear to each of us that our faces had turned pale. A girl, a woman, had risen to greet us, and we had just kept sitting as though we were turned to stone, didn't get up, didn't greet her in return, didn't say anything, didn't do anything. They must have thought us rustic, uncivilised barbarians, even Asit Mitra from Calcutta couldn't help us save face.

I cannot describe how heartbroken we were.

The next day the three of us went back there to return the umbrella. The servant escorted us into the drawing room... then Mona Lisa it was who came into the room. We jumped to our feet to greet her. I smiled and said, 'The umbrella...' 'Oh... Just for this... Do sit down.' That was how I had imagined the scene, but of course it turned out differently. The servant came again to take the umbrella and disappeared. He didn't return, nor did anyone else appear. We stood there for a while and then left silently, our heads bowed. None of us could so much as look at any of the others.

No, no. In that beautifully done up room, where every corner glittered in the sparkling white light, where the most extraordinary girl in the world leafed through a thick book, there was no room for us. But what of that? Mona Lisa was, after all, Mona Lisa.

The rain came pelting down, overcast morning, overcast rumbling afternoons, moist blue moonlit nights. After fifteen days of almost incessant rain, the first day that the sun came out, so did we: to discover the car of the best known doctor in town parked before Tara Kutir.

I asked Hitangshu, 'Someone ill in your family?'

'Not at all!'

In their family then? The question was felt without it being articulated. The next day Hitangshu announced grimly, 'Someone's ill in their family.'

'Who?'

'She is.'

'She is!'

That day too we saw the famous doctor's car, the next day both in the morning and in the evening. Couldn't we call on them, ask after them, do something? We began to loiter near their home, concealed by the doctor's car. The doctor emerged, accompanied by Mr Dey. He didn't spot us at first, but when he did, he said, 'Could you go inside, Mrs Dey wants to say something.'

Mrs Dey was standing on the top step of the stairway that led to the front veranda. Asit paused, a step below her, and said, 'You asked for us, mashima?' These Calcutta boys could use these terms with ease, I was never ever be able to.

Mrs Dey said hoarsely, 'Taru is ill.'

'What's the matter?'

'Typhoid.' She uttered that horrifying word softly and said, 'It's terrible.'

Asit said, 'Don't worry, we'll take care of everything.'

'Can you, can you please? She's my only child...' Her eyes brimmed with tears.

Mona Lisa, you never knew, you'll never know how good it felt, how happy we were, back during the monsoon of '27, in old Paltan, day after day, night after night, during the fever, the fervour, in the milling darkness, the chilling shadows. For one and a half months you lay in bed, for one and a half months you were ours. For one and a half months that steady rhythm of happiness never once stopped beating in our hearts. Your father went to office, peeped in once he returned from work, then deposited himself on his easy chair; your mother had no respite all day, but she couldn't go on through the night, she fell asleep on a camp cot in your room; and we took turns to stay up all night, sometimes two of us together, once in a while all three, but usually one of us by himself. And it was I who savoured most the joy of staying up by your side, all by myself – Asit rushed around all day, Hitangshu too. The nearest place to get ice was a mile away, the medicine shop was twice as far, the doctor lived three and a half miles away – some days Asit went back and forth ten times or more, his clothes, wet with rain, drying on him; another time Hitangshu went off at twelve thirty at night for ice, the shops were all shut, the station lifeless, by the time he could get to the ice depot by the river, wake the people there and return with the ice, it was two in the morning. I would keep checking how much of the ice in the icebag had turned to water, while Asit collected the fragments of ice scattered around the bathroom. Because I didn't know how to ride a bicycle I couldn't do any of the running around. I hovered near your mother, helped her out with whatever she needed, poured out the medicine, noted the temperature, carried the doctor's bag when he came and when he left. Then evening fell, then came the night, an ocean of darkness outside, in that ocean floating you and I in a dimly lit boat – you will never know any of that, Mona Lisa.

All day and night, Mona Lisa lay on her bed, only half conscious, raving sometimes – so softly you could barely make out what she was saying – but the few words that we could decipher were stored away lovingly in our hearts. Whatever one of us heard simply had to be shared with the other two; whenever we had a spare moment at this busy time, the three of us passed those words around, like three misers gloating over their jewels in a closed room at the dead of night. If she said 'Oh' it put a flutter in our hearts like the sound of a flute; if she said 'Water' it made all the waters of the rivers brim over within us.

One night, Hitangshu had gone home, Asit was asleep on a mattress on the veranda, only I was awake. A candle burnt on the table, large shadows trembled on the walls: the light seemed to be giving up its unequal struggle with the darkness. I couldn't battle sleep either. Like a pirate, that sleep hacked away my hands and legs, my body melted like wax, every time I whipped myself into not submitting, an enormous wave rose from the depths. As I drowned I mused, Mona Lisa, are you too fighting death this way, is death drawing you in like sleep, still you're here, how are you here! As soon as this thought came, unbidden, sleep left me, I sat up straight, gazed at your face in that faint light, shadows trembling; that silent moment of greatness at four in the morning. Were you going to die? There was no answer on your face. Were you asleep or awake? No answer. Yet I kept looking, I felt I would surely get the answer, get it from your face, your expression, your voice. And I watched in amazement your eyes open slowly as if in response, widened, after wheeling around wildly they settled on me, your throat acquired a voice: 'Who is it?'

I quickly applied the ice bag to her head.

'Who are you?

'It's me.'

'Who?'

'Bikash.'

'Ah, Bikash. Bikash, is it day or night?'

'Night.'

'Won't the sun rise?'

'Yes, very soon.'

'All right. Can I sleep now?'

I put my hand on her forehead.

'Ah, that feels good.'

'Sleep,' I said.

'You won't go away, will you?'

'No.'

'You won't, will you?'

'No.'

You fell asleep, and outside birds began calling. The sun rose. Raving, fever-induced raving, but let it remain mine, mine alone. I didn't tell the other two about this exchange, perhaps they too had things of their own which they'd hidden and I didn't know, which no one else knew. You, Mona Lisa, never got to know, never will know.

Then, finally, you got well. This was good news, but as for us, we lost our vocation. On the Sunday that your mother invited us to lunch, about a fortnight after you ate your first full meal, I for one felt that it was our farewell party.

And yet, why? We could now visit any time, spend time there, play gramophone records for Mona Lisa, plump up the pillows behind her back when she was tired. In the meanwhile, in the sky the white clouds played with the dark, the blue spread itself in between. As soon as autumn arrived they took their daughter off to Ranchi to convalesce, and even then, from the packing to seeing them off on the steamer at Narayanganj, we were with them all through.

When the image of Mona Lisa standing on the first-class deck, holding the rail, had faded, I remembered we hadn't taken the Deys' address in Ranchi. I wanted to write a letter as soon as we got home and post it, but I just couldn't.

Asit said, 'She's the one who should write first.'

'But will she?' said Hitangshu despondently.

'Why not, what's so difficult about writing a letter?'

Who knew what was so difficult, but even twenty days later there was no letter, though a money order for the rent came, addressed to Hitangshu's father. We decided to get the address off the money order and write; there seemed no logic to showing our indignation by not writing just because she hadn't. She was weak, perhaps she hadn't mended properly yet – it was proper for us to find out how she was. But how would we address her in the letter? Which form of 'you' would we use, the formal or the familiar? Of course, she used the familiar form with us, so did we, but how many words had we actually exchanged, surely not so many as to warrant using the same form in writing, gleaming in ink? Besides, what would we write? How are you, all well? That was all we had to say. A lot could be written if we were to talk about how we were, what we were up to, but was Mona Lisa eager to know about us?

When prolonged discussions led to no solution, the other two finally told me to compose our letter. I was chosen since I wrote poetry.

Perspiring that night by the lantern, I prepared a draft. Using a formal way of addressing people that didn't require using their name, the letter said that we had expected a letter, but that there was none. Twenty-one days had gone by in expectation. Ranchi was wonderful, was it? Of course, it was good if it was, we were happy if that was the case. The ground floor of Tara Kutir was locked up, so old Paltan is dark. There used to be a Petromax light there every evening, you see. Never mind all that, we were conjuring up images of Ranchi. Hills, jungles, red gravel roads, dark-skinned locals. Laughter, joy, health. What an awful illness – might there never be another. But even without anyone falling ill, could it not be arranged so that we could be put to work? Honestly, we couldn't cope with a life of indolence, the days were dragging. If a letter were to come, at least we'd have to write again, there would be something to do. Our greetings to your parents.

I couldn't write more without getting myself extricated in the 'you' problem. Even this small effort had taken till three in the morning. A look at the paper showed this handful of words, amidst all that were scratched out, twinkling like the sunlight in a darkened jungle. I read our missive several times; I felt it was quite good, the very next moment I felt, how dreadful, tear it up. I tore it up too, but before that I copied it onto a nice clean sheet, and the next day we affixed our respective signatures and posted that perfect letter with a prayer.

Dhaka to Ranchi, Ranchi to Dhaka. Four or five days...

all right, six. But no, no letter. Fog in the evening, a little cold. No letter. Summer flowers gave way to winter ones; no letter.

A letter came eventually, or not a letter but a scanty postcard, addressed to Hitangshu and written by her mother. She conveyed Bijoya greetings to dear Hitangshu, Asit and Bikash, the news was that their days in Ranchi were drawing to a close, they would be back soon, if Hitangshu could get their house unlocked and swept and cleaned this would be a big help. The keys were with his father. And finally, she wrote, Toru was mostly recovered now, she spoke of us sometimes.

She spoke of us sometimes. And our letter? Not even the closest of scrutinies of that postcard revealed any evidence that our letter had arrived. What had happened to it? But where was the time to think of all that – we had to get to work immediately. Within a day we converted the dust-laden ground floor of Tara Kutir into a state so spick and span you could see your face reflected on the floor. Another postcard a few days later: 'Returning on Sunday, come to the station.' Only as far as the station? Off we went to Narayanganj.

Oh, how beautiful Mona Lisa looked, in a pale green sari with a red border, a ruddy glow on her face. She was a little less thin, probably taller too. Lest it became obvious that she was now taller than I was, I stood at a distance, while Hitangshu ran around for lemonade and ice, and Asit harried the porters to get the enormous pieces of luggage loaded onto the train.

Mrs Dey said, 'Why don't you get into this compartment?'

'No, no, how can we... the other one...'

'Come along, come along...' said Mr Dey and paid the extra fare to the guard.

Narayanganj to Dhaka. It seemed the happiest time of our lives had been waiting to be realised, all these days, in these forty-five minutes. Ignoring the first-class cushions, we sat on the luggage; the advantage was that we could see everyone. Mona Lisa was happy, her mother was happy, her father was happy, and as we saw them happy we too were filled with happiness. All that had been inhibited and suppressed in us became free at last, all that we had wished for was realised – we made a real din as we travelled, the huge train seemed to be impelled by the force of our happiness. Mona Lisa started calling us by our individual names as she spoke – so many things to say, so many stories – and, as the train neared Dhaka station, she was describing a waterfall when I broke in and asked, 'Did you get our letter?'

'Our, or your?' I reddened a little and said, 'But you didn't reply?'

'What do you think I've been doing all this while? There'll be more when we get home, I'll tell you all.'

Mona Lisa wasn't lying. The doors to heaven had opened for us all of a sudden. The three of us became the four of us.

Then one day her mother called us and said, 'You did so much for Toru once, now you have to do it again. She's getting married on the twenty-fifth.'

Twenty-fifth! Just ten days later!

We ran off to see her. 'Mona Lisa, what's this we hear?' I exclaimed.

She frowned a little and asked, 'What? What did you say?'

I was at a loss momentarily at this unwitting betrayal of her secret name, but why worry now that it was out? With the courage of the desperate man, I looked at her eyes, into her eyes – which I'd never done before. Her eyes were purplish brown, her pupil like a diamond drop. I looked again and said, 'Mona Lisa.'

'Mona Lisa! Who on earth is that?'

'Mona Lisa is your name,' said Asit.

'Didn't you know?'

'What!'

Hitangshu said, 'We can't think of you by any other name.'

'What fun!' Laughter touched her face and coloured it, then disappeared for an instant as a shadow descended on it, as though a momentary cloud of sadness had wafted across her face. She looked at us for a while, raised her eyes, then dropped them.

'What's this we hear? What's this we hear, Mona Lisa?' Our words held bubbles of amusement.

'What do you hear?' she said, and hiding her face in her sari, disappeared with a peal of laughter.

The groom arrived from Calcutta two days before the wedding. Fair of skin, dressed in a dhoti and kurta[7] made with a fine material, he turned your heart into a flying bird with a subtle fragrance if you went near him. We were enchanted. Hitangshu kept saying, 'How handsome Hiren-babu is.' Asit added, 'That dhoti and that border!'

'His feet!' said Hitangshu. 'If it weren't for such fair feet a dhoti like that wouldn't have suited him!'

I said, 'But a little too handsome, a bit ridiculous.'

'What! Ridiculous!' Asit cried out, but no shout emerged for he had already gone hoarse with all the screaming he had done earlier with everyone else, before the wedding. Snarling like an angry cat, he said, 'Have you ever seen anything like this?'

'Nothing like Mona Lisa.' I wasn't letting go.

'Can one person be so much like another? They're made for each other. Beautiful!' said Asit, leaping onto his bicycle and disappearing in a flash. The entire responsibility for the wedding was his, he'd decided, where was the time to argue?

On the wedding day, I woke to the strains of the shehnai before sunrise. As soon as I awoke I remembered that other last night, when I had rescued Mona Lisa – or so it had seemed then – from the clutches of death. The happiness that had borne me away that night as I watched the emergence of daylight – that same happiness returned to my breast, gave me goose pimples. The shehnai brought tears to my eyes. I couldn't stay in bed, I went out and stood beneath the starry sky, heard the conch shell being blown in their house. I went close to where she was; if only I could see her at this moment before dawn, when the sky signalled midnight while the air was clearly morning, at this extraordinary celestial moment if only I could but see her once. But no such luck, the haldi ceremony[8] was underway, she was surrounded by so many unfamiliar girls, so much to do, so much to dress up for – I couldn't possibly steal a glance in the middle of all this. I stood outside and listened to the sounds and activity inside, and over all of this was showered the strains of the shehnai. The last star twinkled out of existence before my eyes, the trees became visible, as did the body of the earth: once more there was dawn on the planet.

That day Asit went so hoarse his voice was reduced to a new bride's whisper; he was so busy he could barely recognise me. Hitangshu was busy too, busy and a little pompous, for the groom and his party had occupied two rooms in their house: he had worn out his sandals ferrying messages between the ground floor and first floor. All day long I tried to help Asit and Hitangshu in turn, but I didn't think I was proving useful. Eventually, when it was time to pick up the bride's platform and move it in a circle seven times around the groom, as was the custom, I stepped forward, only to be elbowed out by Asit and Hitangshu. She put her arms around them and did her seven rounds, I could only stand and watch.

The next day onwards, the three of us became Hiren-babu's slaves. No one was as handsome, no one as learned, no one had as good a sense of humour. Other men seemed monkeys in comparison, even I, his only detractor of any kind, did not feel anymore that his face looked silly. In fact, I began to imitate him, trying to sit, stand, walk, laugh, talk like him. The other two did the same, and this made me laugh; maybe each of us was laughing at the efforts of the other two, though none of us actually said anything.

One afternoon we were listening to a funny story Hiren-babu was telling when he looked around and said, 'Could you just find out where Toru is?'

'Should I fetch her?' I said and ran off.

Mona Lisa was combing her hair on the south veranda, her back to the sun. I stood near her and forgot to speak; she suddenly seemed new, different, dressed in a fresh, crisp sari, vermilion in her hair, jewellery glittering on her ears, hands and neck, and a strange fragrance emanating from her – not Hiren-babu's scent, not the whiff of fresh furniture with its taint of alcohol, not even hair oil or face powder. Instead, it seemed to me that the very soul of all these smells had possessed Mona Lisa's body. I breathed it in deeply, my head reeled.

She raised her eyes, looked at me and said, 'What?'

'Nothing...' I said, then remembered my errand. 'Hiren-babu is calling for you.'

She didn't appear to have heard what I added last, and kept combing her hair serenely.

'Can't you hear me? Hiren-babu is calling for you.'

'So what if he is? Do I have to jump at his bidding?'

'What...?'

Pausing in her combing, she looked at me and said, 'Not much longer. I'll be gone soon.'

I said, 'You'll love Calcutta, Dhaka's no place to live in.'

'Will all of you remember me, Bikash?'

I bustled about, trying to hurry her up, and said, 'No more talking. Come on now.'

'Can't you see I'm combing my hair? Go tell him I can't go now.'

I was taken aback, but Mona Lisa rose soon afterwards, and I followed. I said, 'And then, Hiren-babu?'

But Hiren-babu seemed to have lost his enthusiasm for storytelling. He stared outside through the window, while

Mona Lisa sat on a chair and plucked at the tablecloth aimlessly.

I entreated him, 'Please tell me the rest!'

'Not now.'

I sat on the bed and, leafing through an English book, remarked, 'I've read this. Very interesting.'

Hiren-babu suddenly rose and said, 'This one's very interesting too. Why don't you take it home and read it, I'll take a quick nap. All right?'

I didn't say anything and went out slowly; I felt, through my back, the door being closed. I didn't return home, I sat down exactly where she had been sitting on the veranda. The comb with the scent of her hair was still lying there, I picked it up and ran my fingers over its teeth repeatedly.

One more day, one more day. The day of departure came, was postponed, another day, another. And then they left.

This time there was a letter, one letter for the three of us, in a thick blue envelope, addressed to me, this time. I wrote the reply for all of us, a little on the long side, and a poem as well, which I didn't send. The letters came to an end soon, from both sides, and all I wrote was poetry.

We got all the news from Mrs Dey. They were well, very well. Hiren had bought a car, they had made a trip to Asansol. The talkies had come to Calcutta, tomatoes were dear, but winter had suddenly receded, one hoped there would be no illness. As soon as it got a little warmer they'd be going to Darjeeling.

I started seeing, in my mind, images of Darjeeling, a place I'd never seen, but Mrs Dey wiped them off one day, saying, 'They're coming.'

Coming! Here! To Dhaka! Why, what happened to Darjeeling?

Answering our unasked question, Mrs Dey said, 'She's not well, she's going to stay with me now.'

'Ill again?' All three of us were startled.

'Not ill exactly, not very well, that's all,' Mrs Dey smiled slightly. We felt very bad. Very bad at hearing her, at her smile. Not well, but not ill – what was going on? Yet Mrs Dey was serene and complacent, she appeared to be pleased with the news. We felt quite angry really.

The three of us turned up within an hour of their arrival. Mona Lisa was leaning back on the sofa, a cigarette tin in her hand. We looked at one another – had Hiren-babu's behaviour driven her to take up smoking?

She smiled faintly on seeing us, didn't say anything.

'How are you, Mona Lisa?' We tried to set a light tone to our reunion.

Bringing the cigarette tin close to her face, she touched it with her mouth and closed the lid, saying, 'Well…'

'Are you unwell?'

Without replying, she said, 'What news?' Then she started talking of this and that, frequently raising the tin to her mouth.

Hiren-babu entered and said to her, eagerly, 'Toru, how are you feeling now?'

Raising tired eyes, she said, 'Fine.'

'Why don't you lie down for a while?'

'No, I'm fine as I am.'

'Ah, you boys are here. Toru here has…' Hiren-babu stopped abruptly.

'What's the matter with her?'

'Nothing, but...'

But what? Had she got some dreadful disease that couldn't be talked about with anyone else? And she seemed to have changed, didn't even laugh wholeheartedly when she wanted to. Our mothers had always told us girls became healthier after marriage, but what had happened to our Mona Lisa?

Mrs Dey brought her a small plate and said, 'Try this, will you?'

'What is it, ma?'

'Try it and see.' She took a little on her finger and pushed it into her daughter's mouth.

'No, no, no more.' Lines of discomfort were etched on her face; she put her hand to her throat and lowered her face.

We walked without speaking for a while after we came out, feeling rather depressed. Asit broke our silence. 'She was spitting into that cigarette tin.'

'What?' I was shocked.

'Really! I saw!' I looked for an explanation.

'This must be part of her illness then.'

'She's not ill,' Asit said solemnly, 'she's going to have a baby.'

Hitangshu chuckled in response. 'Why are you laughing?' I asked him, angrily. 'What are you laughing at?'

Asit said, 'That's why her mother brought her that green mango mixture. People like sour things in this condition.

'You know everything,' I roared in rage.

'What's the matter with you?' Asit looked at me in apparent amusement.

'Leave me alone. I hate it, I'm going home.'

I deserted them and went home, sitting down to write poetry in the twilight, solitary.

Hiren-babu went back in two days. His train left in the afternoon. The luggage was placed in the horse-drawn carriage. Hiren-babu stopped as he was about to get in.

'Did you leave something behind? Should I go get it?' I said quickly.

'No, I'll go myself.'

He went in with quick steps, then returned and got into the carriage without looking to his left or right. The horseman cracked his whip. Asit craned his neck, 'When are you coming again?'

'I'll be coming. Look after her,' said Hiren-babu and turned away. My heart cried out.

How silent that afternoon, how picturesquely beautiful, back in March of 1928, in old Paltan. The carriage became smaller and smaller, and disappeared around the bend of the road. We went inside. Mona Lisa was crying into her pillow, her body racked with sobs.

'Mona Lisa!'

'Listen, listen to us now.'

'Hiren-babu will come again…'

'Next time we simply won't let him go.'

'Don't cry, don't cry any more, Mona Lisa.'

The tears didn't stop. I knelt on the floor next to her, put my hand on her head and said, 'Quiet now, quiet now, Mona Lisa.' As I spoke, my voice broke too and I had tears in my eyes.

Mona Lisa pushed me away after a few minutes and said, 'Hey – why are you crying? Silly!' Grabbing my hair, she shook me and said, 'You're a man – aren't you ashamed to cry? Stop immediately.'

I raised my face. The moment our eyes met there was a tremor in my breast, and smaller tremors continued all day, I couldn't forget even in my sleep.

The three of us surrounded her. So that she could be well, happy, never feel upset. If she suddenly felt the whim to eat something out of the ordinary, Asit scoured the city to fetch it. That she would lose the desire to have it as soon as she saw it was well known by now, but we lived in the hope of her new desires. And if ever she did eat something, and liked it, we were over the moon with happiness.

Hiren-babu returned after three months. By then Toru's health was much improved; she was eating, going out, buying new clothes from peddlers, looked fuller. This time Hiren-babu stayed for ten days and then again during the Durga Puja[9] vacation.

But by then her condition was deteriorating again. The doctor visited frequently, prescribed medicines, but from what we could hear, none of it was working. We didn't know why she was suffering, didn't understand it, but we could see its effect for ourselves – she had dark circles under her eyes, she was out of breath after a sentence or two, her face turned blue sometimes. We hovered nearby, fanned her when she lay down, tried to amuse her when she seemed well, but never succeeded.

One day I said, 'Babur took on Humayun's illness[10], how nice it would be if something like that could be done.'

Asit burst out in laughter. 'Whatever else you can do, you cannot take on this illness of hers.'

I reddened and said, 'Not the illness, but the suffering.'

Hitangshu said, 'Really, how she's suffering. She paces up and down all night, apparently – just can't sleep. It even hurts to lie down.'

Asit said, 'That's inevitable. Have you seen the way she looks?'

I protested, 'What do you mean? She looks beautiful, very beautiful...'

'However beautiful she may be, these last few days...'

I raised my voice and said, 'This is the time when she's looked the most beautiful!'

The sharpness of my tone probably took them by surprise; they didn't say anything else.

The more days that passed, the more beautiful she appeared to me; her body seemed to be possessed of an amazing beauty. One day I couldn't help but tell her as much. Last year, when they returned from Ranchi, all of heaven had fit into a small train compartment. On just such a sun soaked winter day, now, she suddenly said, 'Bikash, I see you staring at me far too often these days.'

'You're very beautiful these days, that's why.'

'Wasn't I beautiful before?'

'Even more now.'

Mona Lisa frowned and looked outside. She said, 'You people really love me, don't you. But please don't look at me that way, it makes me uncomfortable... oh, how sunny it is outside!'

I got up and shut the window.

'I'll take a nap, all right?'

A sheet was folded near her feet, I unfolded it and said, arranging it over her, 'You're well these days, aren't you?'

'Of course I am.'

On her face I saw hope mixed with courage, fear with hope, patience with fear. Moving the sheet so that her feet remained uncovered, I said, 'Why did Hiren-babu leave?'

'Doesn't he have work to do?'

'When is he coming again?'

'In good time.'

'Why did he have to go – I wish he hadn't.'

'Enough now, never mind all that,' she said, turning on her side and shutting her eyes. Her eyes closed, she said, 'I'm going to sleep,' and immediately fell asleep. Poor thing, couldn't sleep nights, how tired she must be. I said a prayer, I don't know to whom: may everything go well for her, may everything go well for her.

In bed that night I thought, she might be in pain now, walking around her room, the darkness of the howling jackal outside and seven or eight hours still left of night. Why could I not do anything, why could I not go to her right now, put her to sleep by some miracle? To see suffering and not be able to do anything about it – was this man's fate? Were we really bound hand and feet, with no other recourse? These thoughts drove sleep away, gave me lines of poetry. As soon as I got up I saw the light of the new moon outside; Tara Kutir could be seen indistinctly, like a dream, like a memory. I didn't look for long, I lit a lantern and sat amidst the kerosene fumes and mosquito bites to write poetry.

Every day went this way; sleep deserted my nights. I stayed awake with her; I was her bodyguard, I would protect her from all grief. I imagined myself as a god of

119

sorts as I thought this way, amazing myself with the remarkable lines of poetry that came to mind as a result.

On such a night – it was nearly two in the morning – my hand suddenly shook as I wrote. I heard someone calling me outside, 'Bikash, Bikaaash!' I waited a little, and heard the same call again, in a muted voice. Opening the door, I came outside to find the two of them standing, like shadows, outside it.

The moon wasn't up yet that night, probably didn't come up at all, it was close to new moon. The sky sparkled with stars, the three of us stood in that stardust's glow, on that winter's night, in the field, with beating hearts. 'Well, Asit? What news, Hitangshu?'

'It's started, probably,' Hitangshu spoke.

'Started?'

'I could hear movements, conversation and a low moaning downstairs. I seemed to hear it in my sleep, then I couldn't stay in bed any longer. So I called Asit and came to you – were you awake?'

I didn't say anything. In the starlight I saw Hitangshu's face was pale, and Asit was looking the other way, into the distance. We had changed too in this time, our laughter and jokes were few and far between, we didn't chat much, and as for the person we had said a thousand things about, we were completely silent about her. We were breathless, breathless with expectation.

We didn't realise we were trembling, didn't know we were walking, didn't understand when we opened the small garden gate and stood below the stairs. Surely we made no noise, and weren't talking either, but Mr Dey came out with a torch almost immediately, as though he had been waiting for us. Softly, he said, 'Asit, could you go on your bicycle to Dr Mukherjee, get him to come with you.'

Asit disappeared like a shadow. Hitangshu sat down on the stairs. A continuous, muffled sobbing pierced our backs and entered our breasts; it seemed to have no sound except that of suffering, as though someone had wounded the very soul of the earth. And this sobbing rose from the very breast of the earth, so it would never cease.

We couldn't set eyes on her, not even from a distance; we couldn't go to her room, not even near it; all we could do was sit outside, in the cold, in the dark, not asleep, not awake, before the sky, face to face with destiny.

The comings and goings of the doctor began, went on all night, continued the next day. As soon as it was morning we sent an extra charge telegram to Hiren-babu, and thought, no matter how quickly the wire arrived, no matter if Hiren-babu's heart flew here even more swiftly, he would never be able to arrive before the next afternoon – how helpless man was, how impotent! Doctors, nurses, midwives; medicines, injections, prayers – still helpless, man was still helpless. What was happening, had happened, would happen; nobody had the answers in their eyes, the doctor's face was like stone, her parents had no words except short instructions, her mother couldn't even look us in the eye – and who had known all this time there was a shrivelled old man concealed beneath Mr Dey's immaculate appearance? Who had known these tears were hidden in the blue folds of the sky? And did we have nothing to do besides listen to those tears?

Afternoon came before noon that day, the darkness before afternoon. Then, when the night was a little heavier,

121

suddenly a scream arose from the bowels of the earth; it rose, it fell, it rose again towards the sky; the sky was silent, the stars did not budge. Again, like the scream of the sacrificial lamb before the deity, but not twice, not four times, not ten times, but endlessly. We ran outside, but no matter how far we ran the sound chased us, this was the cry of mother earth, where could you hide from it?

We returned. Inside there were lights, waves of activity, the doctor's voice in the gaps, and outside there were endless stars, infinite darkness, the gorgeous night. But the weeping of the earth just wouldn't stop. The star that was overhead slanted to the west; the star that was out of sight rose over the horizon; the darkness to the east paled, a number of small stars were wiped off, a single large green star shining in their place. This was that celestial moment, that magical instant, when I had awoken and stepped outside on her wedding day, when I had saved her from death, in the only lit boat in that ocean of darkness. For at least one moment that night she had been mine; was that moment again upon us?

Asit whispered, 'What, is it done?'

Hitangshu said, 'No.'

'But everything seems quiet?'

'Yes, it does!'

'Should we check?' Asit stood up, but didn't move. For a long, long time we waited, but there was no sound, everything was silent; then we saw Mr Dey standing before us. In the ashen first light of dawn we saw his lips move. We were so still as we watched, and it was so silent all around, that we seemed to see his words, not hear them.

'Come and see her.'

Asit and Hitangshu did it all, getting hold of piles of flowers from somewhere as well as lots of other small things, fussing around her till two in the afternoon. When it was time to take her away, they were at the forefront. Many others came forward to carry her to the pyre, only I was left out because I was short, I walked alone behind them. Not exactly alone, however, because Hiren-babu had arrived by then, he walked alongside me, barefoot, without having changed out of his travelling clothes.

The next year Hiren-babu got married again, Mr Dey was transferred. For some time people talked about them, then different tenants came to the ground floor of Tara Kutir, many more houses came up in old Paltan, electric lights lit up. Asit passed out of school to take a job in Tinsukia, contracted some Assamese disease within six months and died suddenly. Hitangshu passed his B.Sc. examinations and went off to study in Germany, never to return. He married a local girl and settled down there, who knows where he is, how he is, after the war.

And as for me, I am still here, not in Dhaka, not in old Paltan, not in 1927 or '28; all that seems like a dream now, a dream interspersed with work, a smell interspersed with reality. That overcast morning, that overcast afternoon, that rain, that night – and you! Mona Lisa, who but I remembers you!

The writer's final words seemed to float for some time in the cloistered air of the room, he sat silently before that last unanswered question. There was no sign of restlessness in him any more, he was sitting upright, hands on his lap, looking straight ahead – in which direction, at what, he didn't know himself. All this while he had practically been talking to himself – virtually thinking aloud. He seemed to have forgotten where he was, whether anyone else was nearby. His words didn't seem to have ended even after they had, he kept listening to his own words over and over again; eventually, like with a stone thrown into a pool of water, the ripples of his words died down too.

Then he looked around him, saw the waiting room of the Tundla station in the somewhat abnormal light, the cigarette ash amassed in the ashtray, the stubs floating in coffee cups – saw his three co-passengers too.

All three were asleep. The contractor in the easy chair had wrapped himself in a blanket, this around his over-coat, his snores like the ringing of an old clock. The doctor was asleep with his head on his arm, which was on the table, but the man from Delhi was sleeping in a sitting position, his head tilted to one side; even in sleep his gravity had not been marred. The air of the room was thick, heavy with the breath of these sleeping people and all the accumulated cigarette smoke of the night. The writer, though he smoked heavily himself, didn't like the vile smell. He walked outside slowly, shivering at first in the bitterly cold wind, and then, as though welcoming him, a cock crowed loudly very close by – the harbinger of day, the promise of light, dawn!

A wave of joy washed over the writer. Here was a joy he experienced after decades. Once again that moment of greatness, when there was night in the sky but dawn in the air – that astounding moment, when you couldn't even imagine how soon the goddess of dawn would stand at the door to the planet, setting aside ever so softly, with such a light touch, the enormous burden of this dark and star-spangled night. As he breathed in the crystal clear air the writer thought this was just the kind of a dawn that he had experienced once or twice in old Paltan in 1927. How strange it was that the world does not expand, everything remains the way it is, but only we wither and fall.

He began to pace up and down the platform. There was a crowd of stranded passengers in the lower-class waiting room, some were nodding off on the tea-shop benches, many people had simply stayed on the platform with their luggage. How awful the night had been for them. And that young couple, the writer suddenly remembered, the one that had stood at the waiting-room door for just a moment before going back, who had started it all, about whom the four middle-aged men had spent the entire night talking – yes, it had been all about them, the players and their situations might have been changed in each instance, but the emotions they felt were all the same, weren't they – where was that young couple?

As he marched up and down, his eye fell on them accidentally. On the platform, where the weighing scales are placed, they had found a little nook behind a pile of packing cases. It was a good spot – behind the wall of the packing cases they had escaped both the strong grip of the cold and the prying eyes of people. The eyes of the writer in him lingered a while on that scene. Even in that very public station, they had discovered a secluded, intimate spot; having made a little bed for themselves, how snugly they were sleeping, under the same blanket. Not even the luxury of a palace would have brought greater happiness to them on this night. The light was low, you couldn't see their faces, but you could make out that even in their sleep they hadn't forgotten each other's existence; even in their sleep they were completed by their proximity to each other.

The writer slowly moved away. Gradually the sun rose, people started moving about, in a while there was news that the train would be coming any time now. The entire station sprang to life.

The contractor, the doctor and the man from Delhi emerged one by one, their luggage carried by porters. They looked dusty in the first light of dawn, a little older because of the lack of sleep and their unshaven faces. The four met, but no more words were exchanged – they just said, 'Ah, there you are,' and moved away. They, men whose night had been spent in a strange intimacy, together within four walls, could barely recognise each another on the busy-by-day platform. When the train came, perhaps deliberately, they got into different compartments, as though they wished to erase the previous night. Only the writer kept looking out of the window over and over again in the hope of spotting that young couple one more time; but no one knew which compartment they had got into – or had they stayed back in Tundla? They could no longer be seen, in the crowd.

Notes

1. Large, spiny oval fruit from the Mulberry family, Moraceae.
2. Chewing paan involves chewing a betel leaf combined with spices and areca nut held together with a clove. It is used as a palate cleanser and breath freshener and is offered to guests as a sign of hospitality.
3. A dhoti is an unstitched length of cloth worn around the waist by men at formal occasions.
4. Made in Benares, considered to be the finest in the world and renowned for their gold and silver brocade, Benarasi saris are usually worn on important occasions such as weddings.
5. A shehnai is a quadruple-reed woodwind instrument, used for marriages and processions.
6. Term used to address the oldest of one's sisters.
7. A kurta is a loose shirt-like garment which falls around the knees of the wearer.
8. The haldi ceremony is held the day before the wedding and involves applying turmeric to the prospective bride's arms, legs and face.
9. Annual festival in Bengal involving five days of community celebration, gift-giving and high spirits.
10. Babur was a fifteenth-century Muslim conqueror who, faced with the imminent death of his son, Humayun, is said to have prayed to God to take his own life rather than his son's.

Biographical note

Buddhadeva Bose (1908–74) was a major Bengali writer of the twentieth century. He was a central figure in the Bengal modernist movement and wrote numerous novels, short story collections, plays, essays and books of verse. He was also an acclaimed translator and translated Baudelaire, Holderlin and Rilke into Bengali. He was awarded the Padma Bhushan in 1970. *My Kind of Girl*, originally titled *Maner Mato Meye*, was written in 1951.

HESPERUS PRESS

Hesperus Press is committed to bringing near what is far – far both in space and time. Works written by the greatest authors, and unjustly neglected or simply little known in the English-speaking world, are made accessible through new translations and a completely fresh editorial approach. Through these classic works, the reader is introduced to the greatest writers from all times and all cultures.

For more information on Hesperus Press, please visit our website: **www.hesperuspress.com**